SALUTING MADNESS

I0654605

by

Brenda M. Files

Cover Photo: Willie Files Sr.

Edited by: Brenda M. Files

Published by G Publishing, LLC

Library of Congress Control Number: 2017918089

ISBN: 978-0-9985990-7-6

Printed in the United States of America

ACKNOWLEDGMENTS

First and last, I give all honor to God for allowing me to bring life to these once blank pages.

A special thanks to William and Willie for sharing important information needed to make this dream come true.

Thanks to Gloria Smith, Valerie Bennett and Jayla Cooper for their contributions.

Thanks to all who enjoy reading my stories of fictions.

Just A Thought

Never allow trash to remain on
the floor or ceiling of your mind, deliberately placed
by others, and they have the audacity to leave it behind.
Without haste, excuse their presence, and sweep
all traces of their bodies of works out with them as you
extend words of farewell in kindness and love, while
preserving your Godly character.

INTRODUCTION

This had to be one of the coldest winters I have ever experienced, or could remember in the history of my entire life. However, on this particular night of merciless introduction to nature's wrath of exploding, bone chilling anger, I stood high above the city, looking down at all the dancing lights on automobiles helping to lead the way for drivers traveling along the wet streets, headed for their destination. What a vision of peaceful, and wondrous beauty for my eyes to behold, publicly displayed, and presented among all the cities chaotic noise, even if the roaring sounds could not be heard drumming against the pavement through the thick walls of the hospital.

In the meantime, I began feeling isolated from the world in a room filled with sounds of beeps from life saving devices, gladly welcoming visits extended by the constant entrance of hospital medical staff, who were treating my dying father. Watching him lying motionless beneath the brilliant, white sheet, covering his long lean body, caused cold chills to roam throughout my inner being as I looked down on someone I love more than life itself. Cringing in helplessness, my mind danced in terror, because of the fear of losing him to death, but worst of all.....to possible implications of a selfish act such as attempted suicide. However, I believed it to be a vicious act of attempted homicide! After going over to my father's home for a visit yesterday, we spoke later that night, but the need to see him again was overwhelming, causing a disturbing unrest inside of me.

Arriving at his home the next morning, I rang the doorbell a couple of times, but yielded no answer. This was unlike his dependable ways; causing me to use the key he had given to me for any needed purpose. After gaining access,

Saluting Madness   7

unrest continued to strongly breed wildly inside my frighten mind as I called out to him several times, receiving no answers in return. Walking further into the home looking around while shouting his name once again, the sound of my voice became so loud, not only should his ears capture my pleading outcries, but he should also feel the hysteria from my body vibrating, and bouncing off the walls. Nevertheless, there was still no response as the search continued. Thinking, he would be in the newly added storage facility, tinkering around with one of his many proud retirement projects, I hurriedly looked out the kitchen window to confirm his car was parked out back; pleased by the sight of his vehicle, yielded great comfort. Crying his name out loud once again after I opened the back door expecting a quick response; the wind returned a merciless void, making my heart race in fear. Immediately I knew, without a shadow of doubt, something was terribly wrong.

Swiftly moving forward, I ran to the storage work shop, and surprisingly found the door open; however nothing seemed to be out of order, or missing, except my father. Placing my attention on something being wrong inside the house, and he couldn't answer all of my pleading outcries, I rushed back indoors; like a madman I roared aimlessly through the home without regard, or having a caring thought of his possessions. After knocking over one of his favorite vases planted on the table in the hallway, causing it to crash onto the floor, undeterred, I continued my search hoping to find all is well. In the meantime, seconds seemed to resemble hours during my desperate, frantic efforts. Approaching his closed bedroom door I trembled greatly as I reached out clutching the doorknob in terror, suddenly realizing how sweaty my palms had

Brenda M. Files

become with excessive perspiration, creating the lack of ability to turn the water lubricated object, I panicked. Pulling the shirt tail out of my trousers to use as an assistant; obtaining a firm grip allowed me access into a room I knew I was not yet prepared to see what may be inside, but bravely braced myself to expect, the unexpected. Finally able to see the room in its entirety; no door to obstruct my view; no lingering questions remaining, suddenly I heard a loud scream coming from someone lurking inside, but in reality I was the only conscious person in the house. Rushing over to what seemed to be my father's lifeless body, I tried to gain control of my senses, and not act on impulse by gathering the man I love into my arms; instead I approached with caution, knowing not to move, or touch him. Seeing his body surrounded by a fluid resembling blood, flowing from what seemed to be every orifice of his body onto the covers beneath him, caused me to tremble even more. At that moment, I hurriedly reached for my cell phone, dialed nine-one-one for help from medical, and police assistance.

In the meantime, while waiting on the ambulance, and officers to arrive, time seemed to grow into forever when I saw laying next to his body, the gun he purchased for his personal safety. Recognizing the weapon immediately, I desperately wanted to retrieve and hide its existence for his protection, because I knew the first thoughts of police would be suicide. However, I knew this was something that held no credence in the life of the strong man who raised me. Nevertheless, I also knew no matter the thoughts, or words spoken, these things would not cage the judgmental thinking of others. With this belief, it caused a gripping sensation of nausea to take control over my digestive system; without haste I ran to the bathroom, and violently released my breakfast. Its volume increased to a rapid pace, especially when the blaring sounds of the emergency, and police vehicles in the background suddenly stopped their roars as they rolled into the driveway.

Finally, I was able to gather myself, race to the front door, allow the emergency responders into the house, and calmly escort them to where my father was located. At the same time, with all my might I fought hard not to allow my mind to run in fifty directions as paramedics, franticly began working on his motionless body. Watching patiently, nervously waiting in the background, deeply embedded in thoughts of our loving past, I cried.

Rudely, I was awaken from my trance when the paramedics propped the stretcher height into its extended position after prepping dad for his transport to the hospital; while the police investigator walked across the room to tell me he would be accompanying us to the hospital in order to ask more follow-up questions about this horrible crime. Half-heartedly, I listened to the words being whispered into my ear while watching the medical team carefully attend, and cover dad's face with an oxygen mask as they rolled pass where I stood. In that instance, it gave me the opportunity to caress his warm cheek; with tears streaming down my face, my thoughts became laced with hopes for his survival, because the warmth of his skin gave me assurance that everything would be alright.

Once we arrived, the hospital admission had been completed, one of the officer's began questioning me while demonstrating through his demeanor what I suspected from the beginning, all beliefs were on my dad trying to commit suicide. Each officer had convinced themselves to believe this was a way for him to escape prosecution, for multiple crimes which he had been accused.

Brenda M. Files

CHAPTER ONE

A lone in his hospital room still standing at the window draped in cold frost, it began to rapidly rain down heavy snow resembling, perfectly rounded cotton balls, interfering with my visual of the city's movement; no longer easily seen. Gently wiping away the evidence of winter's frosty obstruction from the window with my hands, trying desperately to prevent the beautiful sight from being hidden, trapped from my view, thinking at the same time how warm, and comfortable it felt being nestled down, blanketed by heat freely flowing throughout his hospital room. Turning away from the panoramic view, I looked across the room starring at my dad, rolling back the curtain of our past life for a few moments, re-visiting days of being his son as a child. Continuing to stare, I became trapped by the thoughts of how tall he seemed to stand in my youth, yielding a great impression that his hair was touching, and just as wide as the sun beaming down from heaven. His jet-black hair seemed to be a crown of glory, a halo helping to protect my vision; blocking the sun from blinding me while looking up, hanging onto every word he spoke.

Becoming completely aware of my surroundings again, my stare continued, but no longer could I see his hair as a sun blocker, or black as a moonless night, now it was almost completely white; just like the man in the picture on the fireplace mantle at his home, a picture of his father, my grandfather. With eyes closed, his head lying against the fresh linen, I knew he was not fighting this time for safety, or freedom for America and its people, but this time the fight was for self survival. With my hands tied in helplessness, unable to do anything to comfort him during this personal battle, I prayed.

Time stood still in the silence, causing the quietness to become so deafening, it was as if my hearing had been damaged during an explosive blast, triggering only a slight humming sound in my ears. Meanwhile, I continued to search all thoughts as to why he, or someone else, would inflict this horrible injury upon him. Leaving us behind, bewildered, and devastated.

Quickly dismissing all unfounded thoughts of personal harm, or theories of police officials, doctors, friends and family, who declared him a victim of self preservation; instead, surrendering my beliefs in a man who never gives up, achieving what seems impossible, often quoting Saint Matthews, nineteenth chapter- twenty six verse; "With man this is impossible, but with God all things are possible." The same person who is being accused of a suicide attempt, is the man who stood through the test of time during several wars, serving willingly for a country that would not serve him. He endured much racial hardship, beginning with the non service at lunch counters, and using the same public restrooms as his white comrades serving also in the U.S Army. He even endured blood curdling hatred spoken while carrying the American flag as a color guard during funerals for fallen white soldiers. Worst of all, were the times he was spat upon as fowl language of hatred came flowing from the mouths of wounded fellow, Caucasian soldiers he helped carry to safety; all because of his skin color. Having God and honor, he continued helping all, knowing hatred was alive and well during those times of troubling, and dangerous situations, all while encamped by supposedly unknown foreign enemy; so all could continue to have life, and the ability to live it. He was a true soldier, a warrior. How could anyone believe, including myself for one instance; he would bring self harm, after confessing

Brenda M. Files

salvation, accepting the call to spread the gospel of Jesus Christ?

Walking over to his bedside, pulling up a chair to be closer to him, and before collapsing from exhaustion; gently stroking his forehead, I wondered where my siblings could be during these times of being needed the most, believing our personal thoughts shouldn't matter, because in the end he is still the man who helped give life, and successfully raise us. Their vacancy gave me many, cringing chills. Each of my siblings had decided to side with our mother, due to the growing blame toward our dad for the demise of their marriage, family separation, and rumors of infidelity.

However, many years later, little did we know just how much pregnancy, and the birth rate of infidelity would manufacture its rapid growth in our lives. Adultery created taxing, and toxic problems in our home, causing many valleys of deep, ill willed, divisions between all of us: permitting deceptive lies to become increasingly ravenous, elevating the volume on betrayal, divorce, and even death.

Nevertheless, for the sake of public appearance, we learned to live under an umbrella of dark clouds, a rainfall of pretend happiness.

Much disagreement rose between me and my siblings, because of the strong stances I had in our father's innocence, leaving all of us with many days of grievance.

Regardless, I remained close to my mother, never allowing anything to interrupt our love for one another, but unfortunately, her persistence about me being in denial concerning my father's guilt, and his crimes driving him to suicide, started a growth of malignancy, reducing our visits with one another to a minimal. My mother believed it was evident my dad was trying to escape from the possibility of spending the rest of his life in prison, or death by lethal injection. Humbly disagreeing, I wondered how could she not believe in the innocence of a man, whom she loved and was once her husband? Especially knowing the purity, and honesty of his nature. Without answering my question, mother would always change subjects, only addressing how the association between me, and my father would be devastating toward my future; especially since everyone has ostracized him on the belief of his guilt. Evidently, she had forgotten to pull out of the pool of gossiping sewage long enough to realize, we as family would be looked down on, because of our connections, regardless of our physical distance. I wanted her to realize, people will believe negativity about us, even if we didn't live under the same roof, making each of us guilty by association, without a trial.

Appreciating her motherly concern for my welfare, respectfully declining any words of staying away from the heart of the matter; I chose to follow my own mind. Accepted, or not in the worlds way of thinking, I became comfortable in the my own belief, while getting use to being alone. I have always been proud to stand strong next to my father, and forever will be.

Born in the South, living in a run down, two room shack with an old rusty tin roof and missing floorboards, the family was very poor with little food to eat, but on most days their mother, a strong woman, would find ways to help provide for the family, creating ways for steam to rise from underneath the lid of a pot on top of the stove, cooking something that smelled delicious and taste even better. Meanwhile, the baking of bread was in the oven, overwhelming our senses with hunger; yielding thoughts of eating.....one more day. During those difficult times, my

Brenda M. Files

grandparents faith in God gave them the strength to support their six children, as well as themselves. Faith in God, love, and unity on their side, life became less painful for the Mallory family. However, tragedy began to strike often; penetrating their family structure as death consumed one family member after another, taking everyone except him, his dad, and two sisters in a short period of time.

Being the oldest child, my father had to lead the way by being the praying, honorable man his mother taught him to be before passing away; soon finding a job to help take care of the family, particularly after their father had fallen gravely ill. Life had become very stressful and lonely, but as fate would have it while failing math during his junior year of high school, he would be introduced to a beautiful young lady who was great with numbers, holding the highest grade average throughout their entire class; her name was Kandi Douglas. Having known each other for many years, but never formally introduced until there was a time of need; after being asked, she reluctantly caved in to becoming his math tutor. Shortly thereafter, to everyone's surprise, the two soon became inseparable, and fell in love.

A year later, graduation growing rapidly near, another announcement would soon be made; the arrival of their first child to be born, me, "Charles Nella Mallory Jr."

With thoughts of their future dreams being extremely altered, they hurriedly married before graduation, and my grand appearance.

Originally they had planned on joining the military after completing college, receive their degrees, and enlist as officers in the military. Instead my father left his young wife, and newly born son behind; headed for basic/advance infantry training, fresh out of high school.

Later that year, my mother began attending the local college, hoping to soon follow her husband by joining the United States Army in a few years: however, she would be entering the armed services as planned, after completing her college education. In the meantime, whenever he came home evidence of his visit was left behind; months later my mother seemed to always make announcements about the stork bringing a new arrival to our family. Being a young child I believed in the fairytale of the long legged bird, especially when they came home from the hospital, (after two miscarriages) with Trinity in mother's arms, creating an explosion of gratefulness inside me for the large winged family friend. However, by the time our mother joined the military as an officer, I had become disenchanted with the long neck, feathered bird's audacity of continuing to perch on our lawn, time and time again, delivering precious packages against my wishes; bringing forth Diamond, and a few a years later, Terrence. Needless to say, the feeling of betrayal quickly vanished against the long legged creature, as my appreciation, and love grew for the last two hatchlings, and their feelings bloomed for me too.

Years before the last two arrivals, even before we came to live a military life with our father, a very noticeable change came along without permission to lodge inside our parents marriage. The change would bring on a downward spiral so rapid it caused shock, disappointment, and sadness to become near to all of us. Meanwhile, grief became my best friend after learning we would not be living with our father, because of quote, unquote, 'career matters.' It would not be until I was a teenager, before understanding why our mother lived in one home, and our father lived in another; they had come to an arranged agreement of living single lives for the sake of their careers

16   Brenda M. Files

and the future of the family, due to a strong military policy. It was a steadfast policy declaring, no fraternization of an enlisted person, and an officer. It was a rule accentuating, adulterous affairs, off duty association, or the forming of personal friendships, will not be tolerated between these military soldiers. It is especially frowned upon if the two parties marry: stressing how these circumstance could lead to court martial, dishonorable discharges, or both.

After learning this information, I realized these two people were defrauders of the government, and we as their children, could possibly be lifetime co-conspirators. Surprisingly, I could understand why: it was a dream both had even before they met. At that point neither wanted to give up their dream, or goal; with great determination they didn't. Time continued its sweet transition, traveling swiftly for some, slowly for others, but as far as my mother was concerned, life seemed to treat her well during our father's tour of duty. She was even more pleased whenever he returned to the states, but transferred to a separate city for very long periods of time. Although his kids were unhappy about the arrangement, we found solace in waiting for his phone calls; filling us with the joyful peace we always found when he was near.

Nevertheless, our mom was pleased with everything that was going on, because she had long ago started engaging in an extra marital affair that overpowered all her sense of loyalty to family. Although contrary to popular belief, our father remained faithful, dedicated to their marriage, forever professing his undying love to the bride he saluted, and the family they created together many years ago. On the other hand, she stopped saying, showing, or returning anything in the manner of love toward him. Unfortunately, everything began to really crumble in the marriage when our dad was stationed on the same base as our mother and starting duty as the assistant to a Four Star General, Thomas Laskey. This arrangement would damn our lives into a collapsing world of hell, never to be recovered, causing our lives to end forever as a family.

Time seemed to permit our mother to continue her campaign, placing all blame on our father for everything, without ever holding ownership of her own misguided deeds. Being very vocal inside her children listening ears, I never succumbed to the election of pick, or choose; instead, stood as the man both had molded me to become. I remained independent, following the lead of someone who always illustrated a great wealth of strength while teaching true manhood.

A few weeks later on a brisk fall day and still living with our mother, I remember looking out of the window enjoying the entertainment of the leaves on the ground, dancing in a circle as the wind starting whistling an operatic, musical tune. This picturesque view became a drug soothing factor for an observing mind, listening to traumatic drama being displayed by our mother in the background. My father tried to keep things hidden from us, but most times he was unsuccessful. Unfortunately on this particular day, all hell came barreling into our home from the untamed mouth of our mother sounding off in hateful vengeance. Rushing to see what was the matter, upon my arrival at the top of the stairs looking over the banister; I watched her every move as she ranted about the action our father had taken without her knowledge. Like a selfish child, she had become angry after receiving an envelope housing papers served in the early morning hours by a deputy sheriff, announcing the dissolution of our parents journey together. After learning my father had petitioned for a divorce, even though they had not lived together for most of their marriage, she still blew a gasket. Disliking the fact of being unaware about the move, caused her to slam the door behind the court server so hard, the crystal chandelier that hung from the ceiling of the front entrance way of our home, started shaking, making a clinging, musical sound for a period of time. The sound immediately gathered my attention, peeking my interest to see if it would loosen itself, and fall to the floor; luckily the beautiful fixture regained its silent stability once again.

Without thought, or hesitation, I began watching this enraged woman storm across the hardwood floor, creating sounds of thunder against the solid oak beneath her shoes, while blaring out a song of words never to be published for the description of a human being, or any living creature. The continuation of loud yelling, announcing the concerns of the underhanded, low down, dirty action, caused veins to plump so large in the base of her neck, protruding greatly across her forehead, looked explosive. Her loud, vociferous bellows were unlike any language known to mankind. After sounding the alarm, increasing the volume moment by moment, she soon realized her audience had arrived, and began a waging war of foul words. She became even more animated when my siblings, (The Three Stooges) tried to extend to her, some loving consolation. Unfortunately this contribution only added to her performance of theatrics that truly deserved a Screen Actors Guild award. I on the other hand, remained at the top of the stairs watching, and listening to the performing arts unfold. "Damn him!" she proclaimed. "How dare he try to divorce me like the spineless coward, cheating behind he is!" Unrelenting, she continued wailing; making a trail throughout the house, with the stooge's marching band traveling closely behind.

Finally reaching her destination to sit down, a place where the mindless parade of participants could halt their march, and mark time; frantically pulling out a chair from beneath the kitchen table, she picked up the receiver of the phone and began pounding the keys on the device to dial her soon to be ex-husband's telephone number. A few seconds later, an explosion of communication wickedly filled our home with undisputable hatred. In the meantime, our mother pressed the device tightly against her ear, leaving no room for anyone to have the ability to hear anything other than the vulgar words she released.

Sounding quite bitter, every word she spoke came out strong, wicked and loud, unleashing horrific, free flowing disrespect into our father's ear. Her words didn't come as a surprise to him, but we as their children became statues during our introduction to undeniable, poisonous venom. "Don't you hello me you low down, no good ##!#!! coward! How dare you send some random person to this house to ambush me, and your children? Are you trying to put us on display in your disfigured, miserable #!!## life!?"

A long pause ensued after her ranting, leading us to assume she was patiently listening to his response. Nevertheless, I took advantage of this time by getting prepared for what was yet to come. A few seconds later, quick as lighting, a flurry of cyclones were unleashed once again. "It's miserable ##!!#, no matter what! I know how long we have been separated, but it still does not give you the #!#! right to make such a dramatic decision without sitting down to discuss it with your #!!#! family first!!!" Another long pause found its way among the loud outbursts, but this time it lasted a few seconds shorter than the last. "I'm not talking about #!#!! discussions we had long ago, I'm speaking about right now!" Standing up from

Brenda M. Files

the chair, vigorously patting her foot against the floor, causing loud thumping sounds; she allowed another pause to gather before continuing. "You can satisfy me as a matter of fact you've just satisfied me with the best present of satisfaction that's ever been given! you've given me, my#!!!## life back! I hope you, your new tramp, and filthy whores will be extremely happy!"

I was disappointed, because I couldn't hear anything in response to her accusations, but knowing him, more was taken than given; at this point I'm sure he extended no extra arsenal for her to reload. "I don't want to hear that crap; you can go straight to hell, back to where you belong, and leave me and my children the ##! alone!" Abruptly, the conversation ended when the loud slam of the receiver was reintroduced to its base. Without delay, my mother zoomed swiftly pass everyone, including me, when she pranced up the stairs barely noticing my presence; with her marching band following closely behind. Being the oldest, holding a close relationship with my father, two days prior to this shameful encounter of terror, we had shared a wonderful breakfast: I already knew to expect the news of divorce, and possible drama to fold. During our visit he decided to share some very interesting news with me; many things that happened with him, and our mother during their life in the military, without divulging confidential information, an act that could be found as treason. It felt good to know he trusted me; knowing I would always be concerned about his safety, well being, and would keep his secrets.

By this time, our mother was now a Brigadier General after receiving many honors of advancements, and our dad was ranked the highest an enlisted man could obtain in the United States Army, Command Sergeant Major, but most of all..he was still the world greatest dad. During the course of my travel to the restaurant where we would share our meal together, I started remembering how proud I was on one particular day when he received an honor for his great achievement. It was an exceptional time; just to watch him stand strong, and stoic as the blistering sun glisten against his well shaven, chestnut brown skin, causing it to seem as radiant as the heavenly element hanging in the sky, under which he stood. Even though his eyes were as sharp as a hawk, the sun caused them to squint; but never once wavering from being an upstanding soldier as a small assembly of friends, and family applauded him for the honor received.

Once General Laskey had completed the pinning of his medals, dad saluted, pivoted around to face all who was there in support of him; however, to my surprise his face had converted from the stern look of a disciplined soldier, to a man proudly displaying a broad smile of joy while tears streamed down his cheeks. Tears were something we rarely saw from our father, an emotion he never allowed to be seen in the presence of others. From the many stories told, tears were not even shown after the death of his parents.

Immediately saluting the greatest man I knew, receiving a salute in return, I felt honored, but the highest honor came while growing up under the wings of greatness, and being called Charles Mallory's son. Later in life, I learned his smile on that grand day was for the positive future being placed in motion, the tears were for the poor boy who grew up having nothing, yearning for something, never dreaming to be able to offer a family, or his country much of anything. He was happy; so very well pleased in knowing there is no limit in what God can do. Pulling up in front of our favorite pancake house, my dad had already

Brenda M. Files

arrived before me; ordered coffee for himself, and a tall glass of orange juice with no ice, or pulp for me. A few minutes later I was sitting across the table from my mentor, anxious, nervous, and wondering what could it be that would cause him to trust me enough to make me a confidant. Being seated for only for a few moments, our order of liquids arrived; instantly the freshly brewed, aromatic scent rose freely in the air from his cup of java, into my nostrils, triggering my appetite to become overly ravenous, and aggressive, setting off alarms of high volumes of embarrassing sounds traveling from my growling intestines. Quickly I stated, "that sure does smell good," hoping to distract attention from the rumbling sounds of hunger.

Extending his hand across the table to receive mine, he latched on to it as if it was for his life. Aggressively lifting me from the seat, pulling me forward across the table, while lifting himself at the same time, we shared an embrace, and he placed a divine kiss on my cheek. Finally releasing his hold, we slowly glided back down into our seated positions, giving each other a smile, a look of love, gratitude, and much appreciation for our time together. However, this only added to the concerns I had of what could possibly be going on with my dad. Soon we were interrupted by the waitress to take our orders; once our selections were completed, dad started generally speaking, inquiring about things going on with my siblings. Shortly after returning, almost before the waitress could place the plate of food in front of me, I began sprinkling added salt before tasting, a bad habit that always annoyed him; but on this day after leading in the blessing of our food, to my surprise he did not say a word in reprimand for my thoughtless act of future high blood pressure. Instead, he escorted me down a path of darkness so horrendously treacherous, I don't remember blinking, or releasing a breath while clinging to every word spoken. After making some adjustments in my seat, still devouring food, I heard dad begin to speak on a very personal subject, causing me to stop shoveling bacon into my mouth, even though my jaws were already filled to their maximum capacity.

"First of all son, I'm going to thank you in advance for not interrupting me during the course of things I'm about to say, hopefully you will have no questions afterward. However, to be fair, you may do so if there is anything said that is confusing, or greatly disturbing, I also want you to remember as always, not to formulate an opinion, but wait until proven facts are given."

These were words he has always drilled in our heads over the years concerning judgment, a principal my sibling have long since forgotten. Respecting his request, I simply nodded yes. "Son......you know difficulties have surrounded, and plagued me while trying to obtain my dream of having a military career, but after thirty two years of service behind me, it's time to retire from active duty. The process has begun, the necessary transition papers have been filed: soon I will become a retired veteran."

After taking in a very deep breath, seconds later dad slowly released a sigh with his eyes closed, pausing for a period of time as if he was out of breath. Opening his eyes once again he abruptly said with power, "after becoming General Laskey's assistant, our relationship was sometimes good, but now things have drastically changed; it's time for us to part company...end our friendship, forever!"

Hearing this statement, disbelief spread rapidly, leaving my face deformed with bulging eyes, and my mouth-wide open from surprise. Believing my facial

Brenda M. Files

interruption may cause him to tense up, sorrow became my silent partner. Swallowing hard to remove the lump lodged in his windpipe, trying in great effort to control the overwhelming emotions brewing inside of him, dad fought hard to hold back tears. In the meantime, curiosity engaged my every thought as his baritone voice grew lower in volume when he spoke about the disappointing situation too heavy to bare alone. He was ready to share his shame, his sadness.

Regardless of the tone, or mannerism, I dared not interrupt him no matter how deep my sorrows were for his pain; instead, allowing him to continue expressing himself. "It is well known that the General, and his family have always been kind to our family, in many instances he made me a confidant, personally, and professionally without worry of betrayal." Taking in another deep breath, he released it slowly, but this time without an alarming sound of grief.

"Well, I've found myself in deep, unsettling matters that will be disturbing to you. This information will probably cause you to never look at me in the same manner again, but I pray this will never be permitted to happen without fact checking before reaching your final decision."

Taking a big sip from the glass of juice, while staring intensely at the clue dropping, incomplete information giving person sitting across from me, I hoped he would soon turn the key to open the answers of his sea of riddles.

"Junior, without a doubt, there are many deeply rooted scares, psychological imbalances, and spiritual warfare's going on inside of me, too many secrets for my own good. Secrets are surrounding me that's harmful; destructive for many innocent people. These secrets include your mother, and Thomas Laskey. I want you know all, because my main thoughts are for my children, but most of all they are for you. Right now, I'm about to say some things you may have difficulty handling," at this point when he stopped speaking, I saw his hand slightly trembling.

Regardless, I remained completely unwavering, showing no signs of concern; besides, I felt more than ready to handle whatever would be said, and no matter what, I'll always be there for him.

Fighting back vulnerable emotions, he went on to tell me about Margaret (Peggy) Laskey, the general's wife, and the strange phone call he received one day concerning the constant absence of her husband.

"Answering the phone, and before releasing a word, she quickly delivered me a long greeting," "Hello Charles, this is Peggy Laskey, how are you doing today?"

"I'm well thank you, and how are you Mrs. Laskey?"

During this period of politeness, I decided to have a seat; waiting to hear the reason for the phone call, and justification for our communication.

"I've been looking for Thomas, but it seems as if he is not in the office today, it also seems as if he has become a regular at vanishing from the face of the earth for many unaccountable hours each day. Now, since I've finally connected with you, maybe there is hope to possibly find my husband. Charles, will you please point me in the direction of where he can be located, because sometimes you're just as hard to find?"

Feeling sad that I would not be able to help, because truly I had no idea where the General was at that point, I stated in honesty "I'm so sorry Peggy you've been having problems locating your husband, but if it will make you feel any better, the General has not been available all morning

Brenda M. Files

for anyone. However, I'll make sure he receives the message, requesting he contact you as soon as possible."

"Did you have him down today for any meetings, or something of that nature?"

"Mrs. Laskey you already know policy restrictions; I can't disclose personal calendar information, not even with you. Like I stated before, I will make sure he knows to return your call."

"Thank you Charles for always being honest, a man of integrity. I have always been grateful for your politeness, also appreciative of the things you do to assist others."

Baffled, but thankful for the kind words toward me, I asked, "what did I do to deserve such high accolades?"

"You did nothing, but be yourself. Charles, you are a man to be admired, especially when you have to work under the blanket of blatant, undermining, deceitfulness."

Suddenly I became filled with curiosity, so I decided to delay any response, while allowing ample opportunity for the sharing of her thoughts.

"Tell me Charles….how can you continue to work with Thomas knowing the things you know about him?"

"What is it I supposedly know Peggy?"

"I'll tell you what, I have to go to the shopping center later today, the one where I saw you last, will you please just so happen to be there again today? Somewhere around the same vicinity; let's say around six this evening."

"Are you sure this is wise?"

"What's wrong with two friends running into one another, stopping to share a friendly conversation. Besides, having wisdom has long since left the arena of sensible decision making for me, so let's just say around six. Will that be okay?"

"Well (pausing), I have to make a few stops near there today anyway, so one more won't make a difference. I'll see you there. Until then, will there be anything else?"

Without another word spoken, she simply hung up the telephone. Suspenseful curiosity was killing me, causing more anxiety than I could have imagined. Arriving about a half hour earlier than the arranged time, I decided to walk through the shopping center during my waiting period, looking for a certain shirt that's been holding my interest. The walk also helped to give my mind relief concerning the pending meeting.

After making the purchase, I took a seat in front of one the stores, in the area we planned to meet; crossing my legs and folding my arms in front of me, I listened to the splashing waters of the wishing well bellows behind me, spouting out sounds in a steady volume of charming plea to quench its thirst for coins. At the same time I began watching all of the interesting people passing before me.

However, at this point of listening and viewing, I felt as if I was doing something wrong; looking at young ladies dressed in very tight fitting pants, or short mini dresses, thinking only of my daughters, and my disapproval of classless dressing. But for some strange reason, I felt like a Godless, perverted criminal, casing young ladies to commit some kind of deviant crime; quickly, I ceased my innocent viewing.

Looking around, my eyes searched franticly for Peggy, but she had not yet arrived, because there was still a few minutes left on the clock before our appointed time. Suddenly out of nowhere, she came up from behind, giving a small amount of fright after touching me in the side. Turning around while seated to greet the stunning beauty; mere words would be an understatements when describing

Brenda M. Files

the beauty of this statuesque queen. Standing there in a waist cinching, floral, free flowing, floor sweeping dress; her neck and ears adorned with gold, Peggy looked as refreshing as a spring day, while presenting a wide grin to introduce her dazzling white teeth. She exude elegance and class.

Coyly, she stated, "Sorry sir to frighten you, but for a few seconds I thought you were someone I knew. Why Charles it is you!"

Getting up from my seat to give her a hug, I played along, while enjoying the cleanliness of her fragrance. "Yes it's me: it's good to see you. Now tell me, how are you doing Mrs. Laskey?"

"I'm good, thanks for asking."

With the acting session completed, we stood there holding a short, but powerfully, interesting conversation. Listening to the information given, I was surprised to learn she knew just as much as I did concerning things that supposedly had been hidden in secret. In the meantime as the conversation continued, Peggy seemed to carry pity for me as she looked through eyes of empathy. I'm sure this was a feeling she held for both of us.

"I don't understand your loyalty Charles, especially when you know my husband, and your wife have been lovers for a very long time, right under our noses. Your wife has had the audacity to convince my family that she is such a righteous person who's been mistreated, and you're a cheating SOB. Worst of all, she has the nerve to visit our home often, sharing time with me, and my family. I can see on your face, you are surprised that I know the two of you are married. Yes, I have known for a very long time. I would have blown the whistle on the crime if it had not been for your kindness. I didn't want to hurt, or destroy your career, because you didn't deserve the shame."

"I thank you; please know I'm truly grateful."

Without hesitations she preceded, "I also know you house many other secrets, most of them has to do with my husband. Tell me Charles,.....how does he repay you? No I'll tell you; by banging your wife. Now you can be released from the bondage he has over you! Now you'll have the same manner of power over him. You will be able to disgrace him as an adulterer, and many other crimes, because I have all that's needed to prove his criminal behavior."

In the next moment, she unexpectedly handed me a couple of very large envelopes; ones she had been pressing tightly against her breasts. After looking inside the belly of one, the first thing I saw were photos of our spouses, clad in indecent, compromising positions. Briefly glancing through the contents, I could also see much more than I truly wanted to know. Peggy had a landfill of dangerous, damning information against several powerful people, besides her husband. Information she shouldn't have in her possession. These records would give support to the innocent who had strong voices no one wanted to hear, because no one wanted to listen. I didn't know how she came to possess such power, but believed she was very afraid of it.

A few moments later, Peggy allowed me to know about the private investigator she hired to follow Thomas as she continued to rant. "Little does Kandi, your cheap tramp of a wife know, she's not the first person my husband has strayed with, and certainly won't be the last. Unfortunately, the strangest thing about all of this insanity is, I still love.....that no good son-of- nothing."

Emotional, tears began to flow as her words became broken while trying desperately to speak, but every sound released was interrupted by quick intakes of breaths, and sniffles, sounding as if she was searching for lost oxygen. Softly patting my arm while slowly walking away she said, "I'll talk with you later," then vanished from my sight ducking inside one of the many stores, looking for an available exit to the parking lot. A few weeks later, it was reported that someone found Peggy outside of her car, dead from what was thought to be an apparent suicide.

CHAPTER TWO

After sharing this encounter with me, my father looked up from the lukewarm cup of coffee, no longer resembling a stoic, physically built, roman gladiator, but a man beaten down, broken and worn. Even though I never said a mumbling word while listening to all of the pains, and woes happening in his life, I became more broken than I could ever remember, drawing me even closer to my father.

"Son, time seemed to corrode through every fiber of my weakened body; feeling the weight of secrets crumbling my existence, and enemies pressing on every hand. This out of control situation has made it hard to locate a map directing me to normal; making life for me, no longer life."

Pausing for a few moments, allowing the waitress to refill his cup, he remained silent until the young lady was out of hearing range, before he continued. Shortly thereafter, he picked up the cup, took a sip of the content, and wrapped both hands around the warm container. It left me not knowing if he did this to feel the heat from the cup because of cold hands, or to allow added moments to think about what he would say next. Whatever the reason may be, I was anxious to hear more. About five minutes later, he began sharing the last words of bone chilling, disturbing testimony.

"Son, if anything should suddenly happen to me, not of natural cause, please go to the bank I deal with, retrieve all documents from the safety deposit box, take everything inside its belly, including any, and all monies: you'll find housed inside, a multitude of papers, recordings, pictures, and videos that will be very disturbing, including indecent pictures of your mother.....so be prepared. These will be documented information and diaries needed for proof and protection for all concerned."

Afterwards, he paid the bill, parted from my company with plans to talk later, but never about our conversations held on that day.

Since that time my parents had divorced, dad has retired from the military, and life has once again become calm for all of us. That was…until the day I found him lying in a pool of blood, now lying in a bed unaware he is alive. From the day of his admittance into the hospital, nothing has kept me away, or made me leave his bedside. Grateful to be continuing my work while spending time at the hospital; more than thankful for a boss who has been compassionate, and understanding, has prevented me from finding words to express my appreciation. However, deep down inside I knew where all the thanks belonged, and who was sustaining me; it's through His grace, and mercy.

Unfortunately, a few days later in the early hours of the morning, I had to leave him alone for awhile; headed for the bank to retrieve what has been in safety, for my eyes only. Once emptied, all contents had been obtained from the safety deposit box, I hurriedly made my way back to the hospital. Inside my father's room again, I walked over to the large window, stood in front of it looking down, watching people for a short period as they busily walked along the sidewalk, and drove by in their cars heading to places unknown to me. Reluctant to execute my dad's request, I allowed a great amount of time to lapse before finally sitting down in the reclining chair, and slowly peel open the large envelopes filled with the unknown. At that point I had no idea of the staggering amount of intriguing, wicked secrets the large storage containers held inside their guts waiting to be introduced to the world.

Saluting Madness   33

Dressed in gray sweatpants, white tee-shirt, and socks, sitting Indian style in the chair I always gravitated toward, located in the darkest corner of his hospital room, my small place of seclusion; prepared for comfort before beginning the long, adventurous trail of mystery, I began reading through the information. However, nothing could have prepared me for the disturbing, massive amount of ugliness; not even my dad's warnings as I read the most powerful, documented manuscripts and Thomas well kept, detailed diaries of evil. Wicked things I'd ever seen before. It was information Peggy had retrieved without permission; leaving behind copies for my father, now inherited by me.

"My dear Charles, if you are reading this, it could only mean one of two things, life for me has either turned the corner to death, or I'm physically unable to care for myself. If it is the latter, please do not keep me alive, especially if there is nothing left for medical professionals to do for me. I have dreaded, and never wanted to be a burden to anyone, so if the disability has you trying to cling to me, please let go. Remember, God has never made a mistake, and please know I am sorry for everything."

At that moment I cringed to even think that my father knew his life was in some sort of danger, confirming this was no act of self harm; prompting me to especially want to read stories written in the diary of Thomas.

"I have no idea how to start, but nothing is better than the beginning. Once I made rank of Command Sergeant Major, working as my assistant, things in our lives started to drastically change. Every day I walked around cautiously; constantly looking over my shoulders because of the feeling of being followed, but when I turned no one was ever present. Throughout the years, your mother never ceased in being relentless with accusations, presenting me to all that would

Brenda M. Files

listen as a low life, callus, adulterous bully. She turned all, particularly my children, against me to divert attention from her personal, tumultuous life of lies.

Kandi is very masterful whenever it comes to deceitful missions, accomplishing them with ease. Contrary to popular belief, I've never since the day we wedded, cheated on, or took our vows for granted. Unfortunately, my naive trusting behind, learned her lover was my boss far too late. Although the pain has been great, for some reason I'm still in love with her; more than willing to forgive her for everything. However, the betrayal done by the person I've assisted, respected and never wavered in my loyalty all these years, right, or wrong, can never be forgiven, or trusted again.

During my first years with the General, stationed in North Carolina, at Fort Smallwood, I learned unwillingly about his affair with another lady besides your mother, a woman by the name of Diane Baker, a Lieutenant in the United States Army, originally from Oklahoma. Shortly after becoming his right hand person, I was introduced to the knowledge of her existence, soon discovering she was carrying his child. This pregnancy was definitely against his wishes, but she stood on the belief that all would work itself out; never considering the idea of an abortion. Her decision caused him to become very angry with her, leading to the end of their relationship."

After reading theses disturbing words of how evil could be so evil, I decided to interchange from the manuscript to read some of the passages from the warped thinking of Thomas diary of madness.

"Diane was distraught about me not wanting the child she was carrying, and granting her absolutely no communication with me any longer, soon she started to seek ways to get revenge against me, her ex-lover.

One night in particular after several weeks had passed, she waited outside the military base at the plush, upscale lounge where gentlemen officer's hung out, a place where I often went after work to relax with other commanders. A place where the temptation of women was not available to me, but never far from my mind. Once my car was parked in one of the empty spaces in the darkness, with only dimness from an old streetlamp to shed visibility; fading in its ability to shine light for safety and viewing. I was totally unaware, or noticed her parked car in the lounge parking lot awaiting my arrival as I prepared myself for a night of drinking and socializing.

Getting out of her car dressed in a vivid, red pant suit, accented by a white blouse underneath; her long hair flowing freely down her back as she rapidly approached the vehicle without being noticed, because my attention was focused on something in the passenger seat. Releasing rage, she aggressively pounded her fist on the front driver's side of the car window, yielding great fright; gaining my undivided attention when she commanded, "get out of the car!"

Trying to remain calm in her uninvited presence, I rolled down his window while pretending to welcome her cheerfully.

"Hello Diane! You scared me half to death."

"You should be scared, not to mention totally dead, you sorry shell of a human being!" she replied loudly.

"Please Diane, control yourself," I whispered while noticing a few fellow officers coming out of the lounge with curiosity drawn on their faces.

"Why?! Am I embarrassing you?! Or is it, you don't want anyone to hear about the non-communication you've decided to have with the mother of your unborn child?!

Either way, I will not control myself, because everyone needs to hear what type of selfish jerk you are!"

Still trying to present calmness, I simply replied, "No, it's not one, or the other, what I want is for you to calm down, think about your condition, think about your baby. Now, if you will settle down so we can talk, I'm sure it would help more than screaming, or being upset. This is the reason you're here right; to talk?"

"I'm here, because you won't cooperate with me. You won't talk, see, or call me back about our future, or our baby!" she said as tears flowed from her eyes.

"Since you are here, with, or without my cooperation, let's talk."

Noticing her demeanor changing from fury to a more calming state, I began doing what I does best... pounce on opportunity.

"Now, if you will please get in the car," my mild tone starting to have a positive effect on the desperate lady's emotions, causing her to soften, harness her anger; soothing all outburst completely. Knowing she was broken, due to the extreme love she held for me, I loaned an insincere smile, motioning with my head for her to join me inside the car. Urgently rolling the window back up as she began walking round the car to the passenger side, I leaned over, unlocked the door, pulled the handle, pushed the door to assist with its opening, allowing access for the unwelcomed guest to enter inside my world. Once she was sitting next to me, Diane folded her arms against her body saying nothing, proving and resting on her stance against me and my long absence. Having great desires to control every aspect of this situation, I took the lead.

"Diane I'm sorry for acting like a jerk, I just became afraid."

"What are you afraid of? Are you afraid of me? Are you afraid of becoming a father again?"

"Certainly not, it isn't any of the above; I'm afraid of the military taking our careers. I'm afraid of Peggy divorcing me; taking the children away, never letting them see me again after we've been court-martialed, found guilty, and discharged from the military, if not imprisoned. Let's not mention the fact our unborn child being held in shame, because of our disgrace. I just don't think you've thought things through, or looked at the entire picture of what we're up against. I understand you haven't been able to really think rationally, especially with your emotions running high, due to hormonal imbalance."

"Is it because, you just simply didn't want to lose your precious Peggy?!" she exclaimed angrily.

Disliking her tone, and the glaring look she extended toward me; angry, but refusing to give her the satisfaction of seeing me appearing rattled, or allowing her to take the lead in this encounter, I reframed from saying anything wrong that may upset her, or interfere with my plans as I continued the act of great concern.

"Diane, Peggy is the least of my worries throughout this entire situation: right now you, and I have more to lose than anyone."

"I don't care about anyone, or anything, just as long as we stick together; raising our child."

"Be realistic Diane, how can we be together, or support a child if we're dishonorably discharged from positions we've worked all our lives to obtain? Will we raise the child on love? How do you think the child will feel among other children when it's old enough to learn about its disgraced parents? Better yet, how would we feel towards one another once we have no money, or career;

knowing we had everything for our future, but decided love was enough to support us? Can't you see what this pregnancy will do to everybody's future?"

At this point I tried to plant pity across my face, but this display did not persuade, nor deter her decision. "I'm having my baby no matter the consequences; let whatever happens, happen." Quickly devising a secret plan in my head for the future, a plan far from being the truth: I lied. "I guess we'll do it your way."

After discussing our strategy, I told her we would have a talk with our superiors, as well as Peggy, but for now, we should go someplace where we can share the rest of our evening alone. Stroking her beautiful black, long silky hair; pulling her upper body toward me without asking, I aggressively kissed her on the mouth, and a few seconds later guided her closer; caressing her body to an arousing point of no return.

Fully receptive to every touch, placing my hands on her upper legs, rubbing them gently until she lost control, moaning in great pleasure, I whispered in her ear saying, "Diane, why don't we go someplace where there is less traffic? because believe it or not, I've really missed being with you." Taking her hand, placing it on the front of my pants, granting introduction to the growing, bulging body part, proving how much she had been missed. Diane graciously welcomed the invitation of seduction, allowing me back into her life as we drove toward a secluded, darken road, a place holding many of our hidden secret, and stolen nights we shared together. Shortly thereafter, we found ourselves entangled in feverish kisses, undressed, and deeply engaged in passionate love making.

The following weeks of daily communication between us, made Diane the happiest woman in the world; happier than the day we met. However, Diane was still annoyed by my unresolved marriage, often reminding me about our agreement of divorcing Peggy, resigning from the military, and moving away with her.

Believing at the time I was without trickery, Diane held no reservation concerning our relationship; instead basking in radiance, but she would soon find out how sorely wrong wishful thinking could be.

A week later, I tried once again to discourage the decision made, but was still unable to convince Diane to abandon the thought of speaking with Peggy, or having an abortion. Failing in efforts, I promised to meet Diane at Charles home later that day, around sixteen hundred hours; a neutral place where everyone could calmly sit, and discuss the situation. Regrettably, he knew nothing about the plan of anyone visiting his home until Diane, promptly at sixteen hundred hours knocked unexpectedly at his door; intentionally I didn't inform Peggy and we never showed for this union of discussion. Charles told me later, after thirty minutes of waiting, and being quite bewildered, Diane extended many apologies after divulging everything that's happened in her relationship concerning me. She described events unknown to Charles with words that were as forceful as severe, unpredictable storms, birthing tornado after tornado.

Shortly after leaving his home, she decided to make an unannounced appearance, at my home; exploding in revealing truth. Holding back nothing, she elaborated on every excruciating detail of private, intimate moments of wild times, we shared together. Diane became even more satisfied in conversation with Peggy when she willfully, and maliciously shared the secret of the unborn creation we'd made, growing inside of her: I was not home at the time, but she was soon silenced by Peggy's angry words of dismissal hurdled toward her. Demanding her to leave our home, Peggy screamed threatening obscenities, "If you don't leave us alone, you will regret it! If you ever return to our home with lies I will kill you, your unborn child, and your vivid imagination!"

Looking around after gaining her composure, Peggy noticed she had gained our neighbors attention: swiftly returning inside, she slammed the door between her, and the wicked visitor who carried unwelcomed truth.

Unfortunately for Diane, pregnant, and broken, no one saw her for the rest of that day; a few weeks passed and she was still missing. A month later, news started to spread like wildfire, flooding through the small city military base, were reports of burned body parts found in an old farmhouse abandoned many years ago. The reports extended to the public by the police were very minimal in details about the crime, except the body was believed to be that of a female, soon producing rumors that couldn't be quenched. Gossip rapidly moved from ear to ear concerning the missing person named Diane Baker, and the fact her life had been verbally threaten by my wife. The police questioned many people, including Peggy, Charles Mallory as well as myself about the murder, but with the lack of evidence to hold any of us, we were all dismissed.

Later, the burned body parts were confirmed to be those of Diane, but after many months passed, the police still having no solid leads, or suspects after countless hours of manpower was put into the investigation: the murder case for Lieutenant Baker and her unborn child was placed in the cold case files."

Getting up from the chair to stretch and give my mind a break from all the growing treachery and betrayal inside the world of my family, I took a walk down the corridor of the hospital floor where my father was housed: all around me were, nurses, doctors and other staff members busied with matters at hand, never noticing my presence. Taking my time before returning to his room, I found the stairwell, a place with little traffic; sitting down on the top step, I wept profusely. A short while later, broken in despair; while wiping my tear stained face with the back of my hands, I realized time continued to march on, and found myself back in my dad's room sitting comfortably, ready to read more of the manuscripts from my father and Peggy Laskey's stolen, untold secrets.

"Son, with all the insanity increasingly surrounding me, leaving unrest as a leader of my life, and Thomas seemingly the core of everything; producing much controversy, impregnating anyone who would listen to his rhetoric about Diane's character, but I had learned how much his lies had penetrated our lives, bringing hurt never to be forgotten. I wanted revenge, but after obtaining knowledge about Thomas, and your mother's involvement, I wanted blood. I was angry enough to kill one, or both of them. I've had many thoughts about introducing him to death, believing it would make life better for me, but my love for God's word, and His love for me wouldn't allow this to happen. When it comes to Kandi's hateful lies told over the years, turning people against me; the same painful shame inflicted upon my life will be returned to her in many folds. Regaining my sense of calmness, giving much thought to these two imposters of human beings, I realized that they were not worthy enough to lose my freedom, or room in the kingdom. As far as our marriage remaining top secret from the Army, I kept all unfounded suspicions secret, private thoughts private for the sake of everyone,

Brenda M. Files

and feeling sorry for Kandi for her delusional thoughts of being the only woman Thomas was involved with, besides his wife. Although I must say, he does have a way of making you feel like you're, the most important person in the world, the first and last thing on his mind in the course of a day, forever pretending to place your welfare before anything else.

Fearful of the possible callus things that could happen in my future, I desperately wanted to return to civilian life again. This brings me to the reason you should know about Corporal Kelly Vines, Sergeant Linda Lane, Private Janice Brooks, and civilian Amy Laskey. These are the names of some of the women Thomas took control of by forcefully raping, and torturing them. Unfortunately, Amy was only twelve years of age when their first encounter happened, she is also the daughter of his brother, Grant.

This act of treachery was the sounding alarm; there were no boundaries for what this wicked man would do, even pretentiously loving his family. After raping these women, he made sure fear was left behind concerning the power he held, and what could happen if they said anything to anyone, especially penetrating and having control over the mind of his innocent niece. Grant had always looked up to his older brother, greatly admiring his fast rise in the military, deeply desiring to emulate his hero; in the end, all Grant ever wanted was just to have an ounce of his brother's love.

This disheartening information concerning the love of her father for his brother, caused Amy to feel trapped. Now only fourteen; still developing, she was a very pretty young lady, standing tall over others her age, but had become a prisoner of her worst nightmare, in a large adult world of madness, compounding trouble by the second, particularly after learning her parents would soon wed. During the feverous display of happiness and new beginning, she knew her fate was sealed in pain, never to be normal again, because Thomas was a part of her life forever.

Adopting worry as an adversary, she couldn't tell anyone about the things Thomas was doing during the stillness of the night, or how afraid she had become of his unpredictable behavior, but worst of all she couldn't confide, or sit down at the knees of the man she trusted the most, her father, because he placed all of his trust, and belief in a man controlling all their lives.

I was very honored and felt highly privileged to be a person people could trust, but when each lady found my hands were tied in my efforts to help in their escape from torment I became a person of humility.

However, after much thought a couple of the ladies, after their traumatic experience decided to go above the General's head regardless of the consequences and file formal reports about their incidents. Needless to say, it was very visibly known they were not believed; each complaint was dismissed without punishment, nor reprimand brought against the General. Although two of the ladies, I will leave nameless, became so traumatized by the military's careless, mishandling of these victimized comrades, they abandoned all thoughts of maintaining their careers; leaving the armed forces far behind them forever.

On the other hand, the remaining complainants stood their ground, never folding under pressure even with all odds against them in a male dominated field of operation: remaining strong in the military. Since that time some have gone on to marry, raise families, even advancing their careers to become higher ranked soldiers.

Brenda M. Files

Son......as you continue to read the many pages I have supplied, I'm sure you'll wonder, even ask yourself, 'why didn't I speak up to help these ladies?' And I would ask you unequivocally, how could I?! when Thomas has my family, livelihood, career, and welfare in his hands. However, after further thought, I decided to give up everything for their protection, but when I told them of my willingness to stand with them, also to report my own wrongful dilemmas, each lady would not allow this to happen. Although, I've never shared the information concerning conversations held with each of them, especially the acts shamefully done against Amy until now, has left me feeling like a worthless coward.

CHAPTER THREE

Working as the General's assistant gave me access to personal, and official information, swearing me to secrecy, but with Thomas having privy to the fact, your mother and I were married, there was no way out of his chaotic web of collusion. Every day I grew more fearful of his evil ways, and what he would do to my family. Even though his crimes were just as great, or greater, he had proof of our wrong doing at the time, I only had conjectures, nothing to prove his guilt except me believing the women accusing him of rape; women the Army didn't believe in, or listen too. Shamefully, all I wanted to do was retire, but even retirement has kept me strapped to his madness, seemingly for the rest of my life.

During the days of double standards, I returned home retired, ready to live a peaceful life, fortunately for me one Sunday morning while attending services at my old home church as an associate minister; after the retirement of the pastor, I was voted in by the entire congregation, to become the new leader of Beulah Baptist Church.....without waver, I accepted. During the same period, your mother remained in the service still waiting on Thomas to ask for her hand in marriage.

Meanwhile, the saga continued to flow with Kandi, and Thomas as they proceeded to release toxic fumes of wicked stench; producing ungodly corruption in their plans against unsuspecting victims. Regardless of these facts, on the last day before officially exiting the military, I went to your mother without an ounce of pride to once again try for a reconciliation, to make our family whole. Arriving at her home to profess how much I missed her; my willingness to accept her continued involvement with Thomas if she

Brenda M. Files

would just say yes to our reconnection. Inviting me inside, looking exquisite in her narrow leg pants, long sleeve blue shirt, and bare feet as she led me to the living room to have a seat, I was mesmerized. After we were seated, I saw curiosity drawn all over her face as she waited patiently to hear what I had to say. Without delay I proceeded to express my true feelings. "Kandi, I came to plead with you for another try in our marriage, if for nothing else, do it for the sake of our children!" Even though all of you were almost, or grown, desperation made me beg, and grovel.

Soon I was shattered by her answer, even through non compliance with words, it was evident by the arrogant smirk painted on her face, while slightly shaking her head from side to side, to show without words, she was not interested in my plea. Finally after a long period she replied, "Charles, out of all the years of being physically apart, our children no longer children, why do you still grasp for a broken straw? Besides, you had the audacity to divorce me, remember. Which in the end, was the best thing for the both of us."

"So I had a lapse in good judgment when I hastily asked the love of my life, not to be a part of me any longer. I acted through hurt and anger, but now I stand here to let you know, I truly don't want to continue living without my family."

Looking entertained by the begging, she paused for a few more seconds before responding; staring at me with contemptuous disdain, she boldly stated,

"Well you see Charles, in order for this to work we would have to have the same feelings for each other. Unfortunately my feelings for you no longer consist of love, the way I feel now, I can't even pretend to like, or care about you."

"You don't have to like me Kandi, I will love enough for the both of us. You can learn to like, possibly love me again, but in the meantime for our children sake, just love them instead."

"That's just it Charles, I can't do this to them, or you, no matter what! I don't desire, or want to be with you." Being very vulnerable, having no inhibition where she was concerned, digging deep within to expose everything, I was ready to accept whatever was to come behind my groveling stupidity. "Let's leave the past in the past, please. With just a little effort, only the size of a mustard seed from you, the rest coming from me, we can be renewed if you would just say yes to giving us another chance."

Highly agitated by my demeaning, unattractive behavior, her voice and facial expressions began to change from pity to an unwelcoming look of disgust; familiar displays of annoyance I was well acquainted with, but had forgotten their existence over the years. Although I was not ready to be reintroduced to these distasteful antics; humiliation being obsolete for me, I was ready to withstand anything, to have a small piece of Kandi. Disappointment soon grew into shame, when she began unleashing disapproval through heartless tongue lashes.

"Charles I've tried to be patient! I was trying to protect your feelings, but since you seem hell bent on destroying every shred of your dignity, standing there begging like an unwanted stray puppy whining for attention, or a crumb to fall from the table, I'll treat you that way. Since you won't pick your pride up, I'll help you put it back on track with shocking truth. I'm not interested in your offer no matter how much more you are willing to contribute than expected from me; I have no love for you. I thought there was love when we were young, but I also believed we were adult

Brenda M. Files

enough to raise a family on that same power of love. But as life moved on we were proven wrong, losing all love for each other along the way, or at least I did......"

Interrupting her negative words that were cutting like a sharp knife, I extended a rebuttal. "Kandi, we've lived our dream in the military, now it's time to live for our love."

"No Charles we have not! We have not lived our dreams since the military became a part of our lives; again fooling yourself. Lord knows we have had enough deception, so much, the count has been lost, now you want to add more! Stop allowing your mind to be filled with fantasies from the past, because this has not been the military life of our dreams. The dreams consisted of receiving college degrees, entering the armed forces as commissioned officers, earn high level pay, nothing less: instead, we lived in a nightmare, hide-and-seek marriage. A marriage hidden like escaped convicts in desperate need of cover to protect themselves from the law, but in our case, Uncle Sam!"

"Tell me how does that matter now Kandi? It doesn't matter how it started, it's the ending that counts. We have been successful in our chosen careers, ones we can be proud of."

"Well...if you like settling for part of your goal, you continue doing just that, but as far as I'm concerned, I don't want anything less than what was planned, even though you are less than my plans."

"If I am less than your plans then answer me this, have you, or our children ever gone without, or lacked anything?" "Honey, I have gone without many days, and nights while you were away for your duties, living on your own, in your own place. Case and point, when you were home on a daily basis, with only yourself to care for, who was left as the single parent attending My children, Me! It's because of Me they have lived stable lives, never lacking anything. It takes more than money to raise a family, honey!" Her voice rising in anger.

"Because of you?" Having had enough; very frustrated with her demeaning arrogance, I stated boldly, "Kandi, you have always been exceptional at lathering yourself in goodness, but have you forgotten, while away fulfilling my duties, fighting for our freedom, I was also carving a way for our children's needs as well as your ability to attend college to have your future. I was the one who sacrificed everything so your dreams could come true to receive your degree, become an officer, not to mention earn that higher pay you often praised. At the same time, I gave my children...." Angrily, she cut off my words, "you really make me sick just looking at you Charles, with your less than honorable, pretentious behind. How dare you find the courage to discuss invisible fatherhood with me. You must really be out of your mind; suffering from PTSD. Well, since we've started down this road, allow me to escort you to the end of this journey; giving the real version in this discussion about My family, a group of people your memory has left you completely delusional about, during your lost years of non-fatherhood!"

Getting up for the chair where she had been sitting, she walked briskly across the large room that was lavishly decorated with the most exquisite artworks I had ever seen; yielding an introduction to beautifully designed, expensive, custom made furniture to impress all visiting on lookers. Swiftly, she approached where I was sitting on the cream colored sofa waiting and bracing myself for anything that could happen from a lady I evidently, never knew.

Stopping short of ramming her legs into my knees, Kandi stood in front of me just a couple of inches away;

Brenda M. Files

placing both palms on her hips, gazing into my eyes with a hateful stare, and displaying a wicked smile. Regardless of her actions, I didn't believe she could bring me no greater hurt, or pain than I was already feeling, but how wrong I would be.

"Charles," she said while gloating, "I have been in love with Thomas Laskey from the first day my feet were planted in front of him. I am the reason you became his assistant. You were handpicked for the position so we could keep up with your every move. I am also the cause of you being sent on long active duties, leaving us with one less thing to worry about. Although I wanted you placed on the front line to be permanently out of the way, I settled for the alternative; adjust to you being in my life. When it comes to the nauseating conversation about My children, you definitely need to know how misguided the way has been for you, and fatherhood! Thomas was doing so well in being a replacement dad in support of My child Jr., I gladly allowed him to fertilize my eggs so we could conceive, and create Terrance, and Diamond. That's right, Terrance, and Diamond are Thomas' children! But being so stupid, you couldn't see in their faces, the very vivid resemblance of his white features. Have you ever looked at their obviously lighter complexion, the texture of their hair, not to mention the timelines of your absences and my pregnancies?"

Well past angry, I began recruiting illicit thoughts of criminal behavior that would lead to murder. However, with the strength of God, and Him watching over me through this struggle, I reframed from leaping off the sofa, transforming my hands into a noose; tightening them around her neck, and strangling her behind to death. I was truly devastated by her honest admission to something I had suspected for a long time about Terrance and Diamond.

Tears began to flow rapidly from my eyes as my body grew numb, preventing my ability to move. Having to come into the realization that Thomas was the father of my children, and how much betrayal had been prevalent in my life, my mind campaigned strongly for murder, and wanted to continue believing these children were a part of me, my heritage. In that same instance, I realized the level of your mother's wickedness, and just how treacherous she had become.

Even though drowning in sorrow, I continued to listen to her spit out painful, demeaning words; still loving her with all my heart.

"Yes, we deceived you! Thankfully, with stupidity as your friend, you gladly took Thomas responsibilities: cover man for appearances sake in the public. Now! daddy of family discussions, we gladly added you into the equation as a postulant mention from me, and Thomas for stepping in; becoming a surrogate to our children. But for me to be a part of a pretend family again, a family that doesn't belong to you, I don't think even your naive behind could put up with such a dumb request after learning a lesson in hard truth."

Suddenly, I heard the words of God saying softly in my ear, "Do not store up for yourself treasures on earth where thieves break in and steal. But store up for yourself treasures in heaven where moth and rust do not destroy and thieves do not break in and steal. For where your treasure is, there your heart is also."

Thanking God for reminding me He is a jealous God, and bridling my tongue, I listened closely to the disturbing details of Kandi's selfish, sordid, future plans of infidelity concerning her life with Thomas; wondering what could have possibly happened to the sweet lady who helped me

Brenda M. Files

get through math in high school, many years ago. Soon, I left Kandi's home and any thoughts of our yester years behind me!

CHAPTER FOUR

Although, not knowing where the truth was separated from lies, I've found it compelling to be safe by guarding myself against anymore hurt; most of all, danger when it involves your mother. I pray daily to live long enough to see grandchildren, after learning the great fear Peggy carried, and now carrying that same fear inside of me! The unknown has been very taxing for me after the strange, and suspicious way Peggy met her demise; never believing she would kill herself, not even for the sake of love. However, according to the MP's (Military Police), her case has been officially declared, death by suicide and with him being highly ranked, the military decided to stand behind the general, refusing unambiguously not to launch an investigation into his possible involvement in her death. This stance and neglect of the army, shaded any beliefs in a system I once stood behind; totally dissolving my dreams.

Unfortunately, I couldn't insist on an investigation, because of horrific consequences concerning my deceptive conduct; leading to the possibility of becoming a permanent resident of the Army's stockade. But thankfully, evidence Peggy left behind for my viewing proves the raping of many women by Thomas; no matter what happens it needs to be told to the proper authorities. Peggy obtained this information during a time when Thomas was away on official travels; searching their home from top to bottom, because she wanted to learn everything pertaining to his secret, untold life. Although, in this discovery there was more than she could, or wanted to handle. Shocked, and appalled by the information; frightened, shaking with tremendous fear, but with a great desire to know the truth,

Brenda M. Files

she carefully read each line of secret illegalities found on his computer.

After gathering her composure, Peggy began a personal crusade of being vigilant, thoroughly combing through everything in the massive collections, about a man she never knew. The next day she stumbled onto a landmine of explosive documents, potentially devastating against Thomas if placed in the right hands. Suddenly while sitting at his roll top desk, she saw a strange looking pattern, underneath the large piece of furniture, carved in the wooden floor. Retrieving equipment to help, she dug open a small grave holding a metal storage chest tucked in a compartment, secretly kept beneath the floorboards.

Nervous, hands shaking, fearing the unknown she knelt down, lifted the lid off the chest, opening it to unveil many dark secrets of sinister corruption. It was a metal chest loaded with evidence capable of destroying many outstanding careers. Immediately she began taking pictures of his private arsenal of poison, for her security, and protection against future bodily harm. At the same time, she tried desperately not to leave obvious disarray among his overly organized belongings.

Once everything needed had been gathered from his wicked chest of insanity and back in its neat and organized place, Peggy knew she was against a wall. Quickly deciding help was needed to safeguard this information; immediately contacting me, someone she could trust. Peggy knew if Thomas thought things were not in order, or out of his control, he would destroy everyone involved in the interference of his life. Regrettably, she had no knowledge about the small, undetectable motion cameras stationed throughout their home; covering all secret locations, including his computer and under the desk; insurance for his criminalist behavior. She learned about these cameras of insurance, far too late.

During the course of putting everything away, she found their supposedly lost coin collection book, tucked underneath the chest. Rising up from her kneeling position, she sat in the chair once again; opening the large binder, turning each laminated page slowly, she found between the sheets of pristine, expensive coin collections, CD's filled with connecting map, a diary with information containing everything he had ever done on his highway of apparent insanity.

Without haste Peggy exited his office, went to her personal computer, and downloaded everything from each CD onto flash drives. In great effort to cover all tracks, she deleted any incriminating, traceable facts she had been in his personal files. While changing the password on her computer to prevent easy access, she began to fear his return home; believing life expectancy for her would be short. Even though sleep deprived, she spent the next day viewing everything housed on the CD's of troubling memorabilia, with highly disturbing information displayed on the front covers; presenting each victims first, and last name, hosted by varied amount of gold, stick-on stars to highlight his levels of pleasure. The videos showed discussions of explicit, egotistical remarks about rapes, and other disgusting things for self-satisfying pleasures, causing Peggy to become physically ill. Hurriedly, she ran to the bathroom, clinging desperately to the commode for the dispensing of high volumes of intestinal waste; also leaving traces of tears on the cold, hard flooring she kneeled on. A short while later after regrouping, she continued watching her husband's confessional against many women over his life span, even before his career began in the military.

Brenda M. Files

Grabbing a couple of tissues from the box sitting on the top of the desk, she gently wiped away the tears that continued to flow rapidly down her rosy cheeks as she watched in humiliation, their lives being destroyed.

Peggy, dressed in a light blue, satin pajamas set, matching floral robe that blended perfectly with her very vivid, pastel slippers, the always well groomed lady of class, known for her articulate speaking, and impeccable mannerism, realized while spiraling into a traumatized state of mind, she had not taken a bath, or changed clothing in two days; learning the depths of humiliation her family would suffer once everything came forth about the maddening truth, pertaining to Thomas, gave no thought to hygiene.

She knew disgrace would remove them from the lives of friends, and some family members, but society would shun them forever, ending a life they had grown to love. The saddest part of it all, she never had a clue. Peggy contemplated going to the police with what she had uncovered, but being powerless, fearing the danger secrets channeling throughout her body, disconnected from all courage, she wept even more.

CHAPTER FIVE

Time seemed to melt away fast, not leaving her much for reviewing all of the physical, and mental draining videos, before the monster she married would be returning home. Driven to know everything, without nourishment, sleep and little consumption of water, Peggy fast forwarded some of the disturbing scenes to help deal with the limited time. Thankful the children were staying a few days with her parents: home alone, with no interruptions, she placed her well manicured, ruby red nails on the key board as she sat tirelessly at her desk feeling ashamed, and clicked open the windows of operation on the computer to proceed once again, her exclusive viewing of the not yet rated horror stories involving her life.

Through tear stained eyes, she read the caption typed in broad, bold, black letters: Corporal Kelly Vines. She was one of the women in a male dominated, working arena, where female soldiers were outnumbered five to one. Standing tall among other females, not only in height, but also as a magnificent soldier; not an ounce of inadequacy, or confidence in the performance of her duties. Vines, one of the most outstanding soldiers to wear a uniform, shining brightly in every aspect, on and off the base of Fort Peeks, located in Kentucky. Young and beautiful, standing five feet-eleven inches in stature, she was captivating; her golden brown complexion was so radiant, it looked as if her skin had been kissed by the sun. With long black hair, cascading down, sweeping across her back, bouncing, and swaying from side to side with the slightest movement of her head, but even when the thick mane is pinned in a bun for dress code regulation, she would gain full attention from many. A ravenous beauty, resembling a run way

Brenda M. Files

model, enchanting even without make-up, Kelly was a person never to place high emphasis on her features, extending genuine appreciation to those who did, only giving praises to whom it belong...God.

Son, I was first introduced to Kelly when Thomas stopped her in passing; quite impressed with everything about her as a person, a few minutes later after saluting in departure, looking into the eyes of Thomas, I knew he felt the same, but in a vastly different way. I remember the moment Thomas turned to watch the breathtaking beauty walk away in stylish grace, wickedly smiling, making sounds of a man filled with indecent intentions. At that moment I could only think, and feel one thing, pity for Peggy.

As weeks passed, Thomas confided in me that almost every thought he had was consumed by Kelly's charismatic, kind demeanor, suffocating any desires for his wife when he arrived home each evening. This statement only highlighted my sorrow for one of the most highly respected women I've ever known. Immediately advising him these were fleeting times, but deep down inside I knew this was not the case for someone like Thomas. Unfortunately for the young lady, whenever he started traveling down dark paths of strong desires for a woman out of his reach, it always ended badly for the unwilling lady involved.

One day, but not surprising, his desires overpowered him when he decided to ask Kelly out for drinks after work, graciously she dismissed his offer, reminding him of the no-fraternization policy of the military. Relenting for that moment, but never ceasing in making his presence visibly known to her, caused her to become very fearful of him, creating growing concerns about her future. Two months later, she requested an immediate transfer to a base in another state. However, once Thomas discovered her action, he became unhinged, unleashing feelings of being defied and rejected, devised a plan of his own.

Realizing he couldn't find a way to halt her request without recruiting unwanted attention, he found ways to deliberately overwhelm her with extra work. During the remaining time on base under his command, all of her daily duties had to be completed, and presented by the end of each official business day before the next one could begin. Eventually, misery without permission, took a seat closely beside her, especially since her administrative duties had always been carried over into next day of business for completion, in some cases, longer. However, because of the new command she had to pull long shifts far beyond normal working hours, leaving her in the office each evening, often alone. Undeterred by this childish temper tantrum, Kelly would reminded herself, this will soon be over; never to see him again.

Sadly, on one particular evening, as she started to prepare for another long night of duties, while brewing a fresh pot of coffee for the rejuvenation of her body, mind, and soul, unknown to her, trouble lurked around the corner.

Smiling, and humming a tune, because she had finally received notification that her transfer had been authorized, and this would be her last night to deal with the wicked, non-sense plaguing her life.

About an hour into her overtime; working in one of the rear offices, suddenly a strange noise came from the front area of the building, startled she loudly shouted out, "Hello!......Is anyone there?!"

When no one responded to the call, worry made her get up from the chair, walk slowly toward the front entrance, hoping to find the noise was possibly the sound of an old

Brenda M. Files

office building settling on its foundation, but also to make sure she was still alone.

After checking, and no visible signs of another person being present, she made sure all points of entrance were still locked. Finding everything secured, her confidence level of safety elevated once again, Kelly proceeded with the tasks at hand.

Shaking her head from side to side, she laughed out loud, uttering in a roaring voice, "silly woman, you're going to have a heart attack being afraid of everything, so calm down, get it together, and just remember...tomorrow you'll be out of here!"

A short while later; standing at the copier, without warning Kelly was grabbed from the rear, her arm forced backwards, the assailant placed a forearm tightly around her neck, disabling any movements, and fruitless efforts to kick, or scream. Swiftly, the attacker aggressively twirled the two of them around, pushing her face down onto the floor; his body weight on top created a harder landing for the stunning beauty. Scared, she tried to release a scream, but instantly a knife was planted across her lips allowing the weapon to speak in high volumes. Visibly afraid, she laid motionless on the cold floor, waiting on instructions to be delivered from the mysterious person controlling the situation, while praying silently not to die.

Surprised by the attackers next move, Kelly believed this was her last day to live, when the assailant angrily turned her over, hoping to find petrified terror in her eyes, was a gratifying reaction for him. When she found herself starring into the face of evil, a face belonging to General Thomas Laskey, her eyes became filled with overflowing water, running down her cheeks onto the floor; knowing death for sure, was hers. In the next moment he said in an aggressive tone; speaking through clinched teeth, a voice never heard before,

"When I ask, you give! do you understand?!" With increasing tears, Kelly willingly tried to obey, cooperating with every utterance coming from his mouth.

"Now that I have your undivided attention, I want you to get up, walk toward the front door to retrieve something I left behind."

With fear lying heavy on her chest, his anger mounting rapidly, the seconds on the clock seemed to stop ticking as she rose slowly, listening to all orders given. Following directions, but seemingly far too slow for Thomas, he began aggressively pulling her to her feet by the same arm he originally held behind her back. Once standing, he forced her arm behind her again, pressing the knife's blade firmly against her neck with his other hand to help in leading them to the front of the building.

Finally arriving at their destination, Kelly became overwhelmingly numb, thinking the worse once she saw a video recorder near the entranceway. After retrieving the camera, she knew this was not going to end well, especially knowing the intent and seeing the identity of her assailant. Choosing the office in the rear of the mobile building, he bound her hands together, making her lie face down on the floor; peacefully cooperating, she prayed for expectancy of life. Watching him set up the recorder for filming of his intended plan; frightened, for what seemed like an eternity, Kelly waited on his next move. Scared, but not surprised when he kneeled down, placed the knife on her leg, slowly moving it upward, allowing the blade to lead the way, her loud whimpering annoyed Thomas, trigging him to make even more demands. "Stop bawling, making all those childish sounds, and act like a woman so you can enjoy being with me! You want to be with me...don't you?!"

Restrained under his power, reluctantly Kelly nodded her head in a flurry of brisk yes motions, hoping not to agitate, but please him on every hand. However, she would be proven wrong when he blurted out in a strange, loud roar, "When I ask a question, you need to answer, not nod!"

Quickly she replied, "Yes sir."

"Yes sir, what!"

"Yes sir, I want to be with you."

"You want to make love to me, don't you Kelley!"

"Yes sir, I want to make love to you."

Disgusted behind each word, she tried with difficulty not to make a sound, but humbly submissive, permitting the stroking against her legs to continue.

Forcing his other hand between her legs, he began pushing them apart to reach her private treasure. Moments later he lifted the green Army issued skirt upward; with the knife tip, cutting through the seat of her undergarments to view, and touch her secret garden. Seeing the anguish displayed, steadily growing on her face, he become even more aroused in desire. Removing his hand from her garden, like a madman he cut her blouse open, gaining access to her bra, aggressively releasing each hook holding the garment together, she listened to the anguishing sound of the unzipping of his pants ringing out in the silence.

Eventually he placed his body on top of hers, whispering softly in her ear, "I hope to satisfy you royally since we've waited so long for this moment to happen."

Now holding in his hand a new choice of weapon, Thomas began rubbing his private part from side to side against her body.

Finding the nerves, she tried to discourage him from his plans, calmly stating in fear, "please don't.....," but was interrupted by his madness.

Using her unfinished words to his advantage, he simply replied with a smile, "I don't plan to hurt you. I will do my best to please you, my beautiful, sweet lady."

Kissing her gently up, and down her back, and neck as though they were truly making love, not a rape being committed, a few moments later he plunged into her private paradise, moaning in great pleasure. Shortly thereafter, he released a blood curdling scream; becoming satisfied with his insane accomplishment. Never having been with a man before, she wanted him to stop, because of pain, instead she continued praying to have life.

Nevertheless, after finishing his planned adventure, without thought Thomas allowed his weight to rest firmly on her body, while kissing her on the neck once again.

Finally dismounting her, he forcefully turned the frighten lady onto her back to face him, and have direct eye contact saying excitingly, "You're as sweet as I imagined! Hope I didn't hurt you! You've made me so happy, that we had this private time together before you left! Once you get settled at your next post, time permitting, promise me that we can see each other again! This would really make me happy, how about you?"

Realizing he was truly a madman; she remained silent; surprisingly he didn't demand a response.

Believing all over was a great mistake, when suddenly seated in an upright position, hands being untied, she listened to the command of completely disrobing as he traced the knife's blade around her breast.

Looking deranged, Thomas pulled her up by the hands, took a couple of steps backwards, smiled with gleam, and clapped as she removed what was left of her clothing.

Brenda M. Files

"You are perfect," he stated eagerly.

Walking forward once again, he reached out, pulled her against his body, aggressively hugging, and kissing her: still trying to cooperate, she responded in a positive manner, hoping not to vomit inside his mouth.

Lying her body down on a worn, plaid sofa that's been in the office for many years, he placed one of her legs on the back of the couch and the other left to brush against the floor, he proceeded to give abnormal, disgusting instructions for filming, with, and without his participation. Being his tortured prisoner, raped over and over again, she did everything as instructed.

It wasn't until around four o'clock the next morning, he finally allowed her to cleanse herself under his watchful eyes, but not before she thoroughly washed his body first. Kelley began imagining uncontrollable thoughts of being found by the morning staff, nude, and mutilated, resting in dried blood, beneath her lifeless body.

Still quiet, Kelly did exactly as told, while he declared in a forceful tone, "I hope our little rendezvous will remain a secret between the two of us! If it doesn't, you will leave this room alive today, but rest assured, your life will come to a quick end! Remember my arms of power have a reach far bigger, and longer than anyone could ever imagine! But, I know you were well pleased, and satisfied! Now, tell me, do we have a problem, or an understanding?!"

Finally saying something, she reluctantly stated, "We have an understanding."

When finally set free, Kelly rushed to the Barracks, showered, hastily pack, got dressed, signed and picked up, the necessary papers for the completion of her exit: angrily leaving the night of horror, the General, and Fort Peeks in the rear view mirror of her life, forever.

Junior, I guess we'll never understand how he could do these awful things without the least bit of a conscience, but needless to say, you will soon learn that the woman you've always loved as mother, will also betray her family in more ways than you could ever imagine."

Brenda M. Files

CHAPTER SIX

Once again I became distracted while reading and digesting the traumatizing words from the painful and excruciating pages of truth, when the door of his room opened widely, allowing the lights of the corridor to shine brightly into my eyes; hurriedly, the night nurse came inside. After our exchanges of pleasantries; small talk session, she busied herself with the routine check of the machines fluid levels, flowing into the body of my father. I used this time to get up from the chair to stretch, free my mind for a few moments, hoping to lose most thoughts of all the damaging words, designated for my eyes only.

Walking over to view my father, I began rubbing my hand over the top of his hair as tears ran down my face. Closing my eyes, without thought I prayed out loud.

'Dear God, my father in heaven, the One and only true God, I come before Your throne giving all praises unto You, glorifying Your holy name. Blessed is Your kingdom, and great is Your throne. Father, without delay I must say, thank You for all things being as well as they are! Thank You for these living moments in a day I've never seen before, and never shall again. Thank You for continuing to freely give love, not deserved. Lord, I come before You with a bowed head, and a humble heart, thanking you for the father given to me on this earth, a great leader of his children. Now I pray Father God, that You will bring us through these perilous times, to grant peace that surpasses all understanding, during these trials of tribulation. Thank You for reminding us that You are forever in control. Father, we are truly grateful You still allow unworthiness to stand before Your Holy presence, always forgiving Your children. Now Lord, take care of the Laskey's and all families of this world, planting all deeply in

Your amazing grace and mercy. Lovingly I pray, everything in the beautiful, majestic name of Your Son Jesus Christ! Amen, Amen, and Amen!'

Unaware, but pleasantly pleased to know the nurse was still in the room when I heard her say, "Amen." Opening my eyes, I looked around to find a short, slightly overweight lady standing by at door smiling. A few seconds, she turned to leave, but before exiting, she said in a kind tone, "Thank you Mr. Mallory, I really needed to hear and be included in your prayer. Please continue to pray for my family when you go to God, I truly believe He heard your cry. By the way, I'll come back later"

Without another word said, or waiting for a response, she walked out the room, leaving me with my thoughts. Pleased with her kindness, I too began to smile.

Engrossed by the sweet spirit left behind, once again I massaged the top of my father's head humming, and singing in a low tone, the old spiritual hymn, Amazing Grace. I don't remember how long I stood there watching his motionless body before traveling down memory lane, turning onto the corner to my childhood, gathering many loving connecting moments we had as a family. Even though delicious thoughts were dancing inside my head, I found it difficult to pinpoint our family's complete derailment.

Regardless, I became more determined than ever, to untie the noose that was tightening, trying to strangle the life out of my father's reputation, character, and career. I wanted desperately to find out what really happened to him. What I wanted more than anything, was to unveil the mysterious plot behind the heinous act of betrayal, and attempted murder on his life. Little did I know how well, and how much my unconscious father, and now deceased Peggy

Brenda M. Files

Laskey, would assist in obtaining evidence to substantiate the mean ugliness targeted against loved ones.

Impregnated by memories as a child, ones stored in the back of my mind, covered by dust, and cobwebs, I remembered the love story our parents presented to us, of how they met in high school, also the day my father left for basic training. He loved telling us how beautiful our mother looked while holding me in her arms, not looking the part of someone who'd recently given birth.

After kissing his family good-bye, looking back lovingly at his bride standing there in a linen, powder blue, sheath dress; seemingly tailored for her body, found it even more difficult to board the bus heading to his chosen, but unknown future.

Finally tarring himself away from his thoughts, and strong desires of turning around, never to leave her sight, he did what had to be done in order to support his family. At the same time my mother stood strong, watching him board the bus, soon disappearing from view, until she finally located him in the back of the racist transportation system, waving from the window where he sat.

When the bus pulled from the station, he threw kisses in the air toward his wife, and child through the open window, screaming out loudly, the words I love you; anxiously she waved back, yelling the same sentiments.

Unfortunately for us with time passing, their love became a shaded farce of pretense for the public; children used as pawned pieces in a real game of perfect, make-believe family life. Years of living under the roof of our mother, we learned how to grin, bear falsehoods in deceitfulness, and never forget not to share what goes on in the privacy of our home.

Finally able to release my mind from the entrapment of past times, I planted my consciousness back to the matter at hand: finishing the business of my father. But nothing could brace me for things I had yet to behold in the loaded, life shattering manuscripts as I once again, began to read.

"My son, if you have read this far, you're about to be introduced to more gruesome documents, and I hate being the one inviting you into this sea of madness. Junior, even if I am no longer among the living, stand with truth; in the final analysis, defend my honor. After finding out about the romance between your mother and Thomas it gave me pause, but the creation of your siblings never made me feel any different about them; regardless of not being from the blood of my body, both will always be children, developed through the love in my heart. To tell the truth, I feel sorry for Kandi, for being in love with Thomas, a man she can't see for what he really is, but fortunately for us, he wrote down, and recorded everything for his enjoyment, including the day he met a beautiful lady by the name of Linda Lane. A very stunning, professional young lady, who just so happen to be the assistant to your mother. Enthralled, by the classy lady, Thomas became spellbound. On several occasions, in the presence of Linda, your mother became infiltrated with extreme jealousy, because of the obvious attention her lover extended toward the glamorous beauty, with unique features. Your mother had become very uncomfortable with Linda being around, when Thomas was among them. Accepting unwillingly, his roaming eyes, thirsty lust for the opposite sex; remaining silent she tolerated whatever would make him happy. Hate became a selfish, unattractive trait your mother inherited against any female Thomas found appealing, she remained faithful to the crazed womanizer, but disliked the ladies more than me. These beautiful, clueless ladies became Kandi's ultimate enemy, leaving no explanation other than conspicuous, unadulterated insanity, wrapped in his madness, protecting her territory. Her behavior became the help needed to perpetuate every aspect of his sick crimes.

One day without thought, Thomas asked your mother to invite Linda to her home for dinner; showing measures of faith, and belief in the work she's doing. The first invite was turned down, because Linda had a previous engagement, also reservations concerning the military rules, however she eventually accepted. Unhappy, about the pending plans, believing Thomas had wicked intentions, Kandi tried unsuccessfully to get him to cancel the pre-arranged meeting, but never vocalizing her disapproval, or revealing her true feelings about his choices, or ideas.

Arriving shortly after him, Linda was greeted with a warm welcome by both of the commanders, although not expecting him to be joining them for the evening, she politely returned welcoming sentiments of greetings. While complimenting Kandi on the decor of her home, and the fragrance of inviting aromas penetrating her nostrils from the meal being prepared, Linda extended to the hostess, a bottle of red wine as a gift of appreciation. After much hesitation and reservations, she finally became relaxed; delighted to have been included in the evening with her superior officers. In the meantime, advancements danced in her head like sugar plums, while saluting and dreaming of plans for a bright future within the military made her giddy.

After sharing a wonderful meal, great conversation filled with laughter, they retired into the living room to continue their enjoyable evening. Unaware of the potential danger brewing inside the house, (that was not coffee) she became even more relaxed. Suddenly Thomas suggested preparing each, a glass of after-dinner wine, compliments of a gift from their guest. The offer was accepted by all, causing Thomas to become overly delighted.

After disappearing into the kitchen to prepare the drinks, a few minutes later he reappeared, carrying a silver tray holding three glasses filled with relaxing fluid, carefully distributing, designated container to each lady; saving one for himself. Feeling accomplished, he sat down in the plush, leather recliner he had strategically positioned in the corner of the room; ready to resume the pleasantries held between them. However, during the course of these shared moments, Kandi became extremely suspicious of his aggressive behavior when he tried several times to retrieve Linda's glass as her words began to slur.

Upon his last effort, no resistance came from the flawless beauty, Thomas hurriedly gathered the glass from her hand before crashing onto the floor, displaying a Cheshire cat grin, granting Kandi's suspicions to become crystal clear that he had put something in her guest drink. Instantly she became fearful, but questioned his action, "Did you do anything to her? Please tell me you didn't, especially while she's visiting my home!"

"I gave her a little something to relax. You know how overwhelming it can be in the company of your superiors."

"She didn't need anything to relax, she was already relaxed!" Looking at Kandi with displeasing contempt, he said nothing. With terror climbing rapidly inside of her, never wanting to cross Thomas, he finally spoke with a voice of complete authority, giving her disturbing, vivid instructions; quickly she conformed.

"I want you, just for a few moments to be quite, help me to get her into the bedroom so she can sleep off her consumption of wine." Astounded by this remark, feeling belittled; knowing Linda had only one glass of wine, (she didn't finish) Kandi questioned his action no further.

After carrying the young lady into the bedroom, lying her on the bed decorated in white linen, and a fluffy down comforter, accented by large pillows stuffed in white cases; fit for royalty, Thomas requested, "what I would like for you to do now, undress the young lady; we don't want her clothes to become wrinkled," smiling behind every word he said.

Afraid to call the authorities; hoping his response coincided with the question she was about to ask, "would you like me to put her on a set of my pajamas?"

"I would like you to put her on nothing but you...then me!"

"What!?" she responded aggressively.

"Are you out of your mind? We could lose our careers behind this!"

"Well, this will be familiar territory for you, won't it? Remember, you have been at the point of losing this career before, stop acting all holier than thou! Just get her undressed, and I guarantee.....you will enjoy this new adventure in our lives."

Suddenly, sprinting out of the room rushing toward the bathroom, without closing the door she dropped to her knees, hung onto both sides of the commode, releasing every ounce of the dinner they had shared together.

Finally gaining control over her system, she was able to re-enter the bedroom, hoping Thomas had changed his warp way of thinking, particularly after seeing how ill she had become. But to her disappointment, he had undressed Linda as well as himself, granting all three to lie naked on the bed. Now, with all options dispelled for getting out of this situation, she decided on a stalling tactic.

"I need to brush my teeth."

"What you need to do is take off those clothes, twist that lovely body slowly over here so I can enjoy watching every inch of you, and what you're about to be entertain me with. Besides, I think the aroma of your true reaction will be the fragrance needed to turn me on even more." Startled, and filled with dismay, she began to slowly undress and move in seductive dance for his gratification.

Slowly climbing onto the bed, she gathered herself on top of him, but was soon instructed to mount Linda, kiss her from head to toe, reluctantly she did as she was told, increasing his arousal, while recording their deranged sexual behavior. In the beginning, only one was a willing participant during this sexual escapade, but in the end, two enjoyed themselves immensely.

With their mission complete, Thomas more than satisfied with the accomplishment; his soul mate no longer carrying reservations, or negative feelings about the event, both basked in radiance. In the meantime, Linda struggled to come from under the restrictions of the control substance, never knowing the indecency done by her two leaders. Moaning but not in pleasure, Thomas found Linda's sounds inviting, leading Kandi to satisfy their appetite of abuse one more time. Throughout the rest of the evening, until the early morning hours of the next day, they raped Linda several times without regret.

Around two thirty that morning, Kandi woke up from a satisfied rest, with the revelation of letting Linda go, even if she remembered some, or all of what happened. Waking Thomas to share her thoughts, he agreed. After giving more thought to their decision, Kandi added, "What will we do if she goes to the MP's, and they bring charges against us?"

Brenda M. Files

"No need to fret my darling, she will not talk once it's understood we can destroy her and her career. As long as we stick together, nothing can be proven. You did enjoy sharing her with me, right?" Smiling behind his comment, she hurriedly answered, "Yes."

Although, not completely satisfied, Kandi declared, "I heard everything you said...but what if she doesn't frighten so easily? What if she doesn't care about losing her career, or life? What if she wants to get even with her attackers, her rapists? You do know we are rapist, right?!"

"What is your problem Kandi? Just do as I said; stick together."

No longer proposing questions, she started demanding, "Thomas, I want you to listen, and listen well, we will not make threats, but promises. We will not just sit back waiting for what may happen to our future, or to hers; for what I have in mind, there will be total cooperation. Now, here's what we are going to do; it will work, but only if we stick together." Listening intensely to what she had to say, Thomas became very intrigued. "If needed, we will band together about her intrusion into my home without any coercion; capping it all off with a bribe in the form of a bottle of wine to complete the planned evening of socialization and potential advancement in her career. We'll keep the bottle, wipe your prints off, and put her prints back on it, just in case it's needed as proof. I know without a doubt, this will work!" Thomas agreed.

The next day, even though Linda did not remember the majority of the evening as Kandi campaigned against the element of surprise at her home during her private time, expressing to Linda, "this will not be tolerated, things like this should never happen again." After listening to the reprimand, knowing she had been invited to dinner, Linda became even more confused, particularly about losing her career, but in the end all she wanted was to remember the evening with her superiors. Promising never to disclose having been within the walls of Kandi's home, if allowed another chance to continue her career, and after she was given stern encouragement to relocate in military duties, Linda regrettably had to transfer to another base. Before departing, she apologized for her misbehavior once again and felt privileged to remain a soldier.

The next morning, Kandi placed a special request for her to be transferred to another command, effective immediately; giving her a glowing recommendation for future promotions in her next duty. Upon her departure, the rapist couple felt relieved they had gotten away with their unspeakable crime. With much time passing, life seemed to regain some normalcy for the duo when nothing had been reported to the authorities, or caused them any problems. Soon Thomas began contemplating in his rabies mind, the next conquest."

Brenda M. Files

CHAPTER SEVEN

Shaken by the details of what I was reading about a woman known as my mother, I started to cry uncontrollably. Closing the pages of truth for a few minutes in effort to restrain my emotions; instead, released a flood gate of tears, I prayed I had misread the pages. Slowly opening the folder, reading again the entire passages of my father's honest, meticulous work, I knew every word documented was truth. Slightly intimidated by the unknown of what was to come next, I cringed at the possibility, but continued reading.

"Dear Charles, I realize these truths has devastated you as it did me, but please remain strong, always love your mother through the good, and the bad, and no matter what, remember she will always be your mother." Knowing what I would need to proceed, dad extended to me necessary words of comfort as I continued with my promise; reading.

"Once I learned your mother had been included in the misgiving of Thomas' sexual behavior, it helped me to realize the woman I was in love with was no more. It also helped me to have an even greater desire for me and my children to become whole again. Unfortunately, Kandi was too broken to mend.

Years later, with your mother becoming the farthest thing from my mind and God giving me a new bride, the church, I'm thankful for her change of heart, and lack of love for me. Her decision allowed the voice of God to continuously be heard, making me a good leader of His flock, also a better father to my children.

During the next few months, indecent things continued to happen that could not be explained, and all was swept under the grounds of the military base. Son, I know there is a possibility you may watch the tapes in your possession, but hopefully these hand written pages will be sufficient. However, if you decide to view these explicit showings, it will be impossible to get the harsh, graphics details out of your mind. I know, because I have not been successful in my efforts, particularly about a young private by the name of Janice Brooks, stationed under my command at Fort Peeks. Janice was polite, but very independently outspoken, who did whatever I asked, without question. She was a dedicated soldier, led by a strong drive to retire from the Army as a Sergeant Major. After growing up as an orphan, she believed stability of family could be found within the military, but had no idea she would meet a General, promoting untrue kindness. Janice was a tall, slim, and a very attractive young lady, with deep dimples set in each cheek, accenting her beautiful smile. At the beginning, and end of each day without effort, she exude confidence, whether dressed in her military uniform, sweat outfits, or perfect fitting civilian clothing, adorning her shapely body.

Upon meeting Thomas at an off base wedding reception for a mutual friend, she became enchanted and enthralled with the stories of his career life, shared with a small group of people, she happened to be among. When the reception had come to an end, the newlyweds whisked off to their untold destination, General Laskey escorted her, and her roommate to their cars through the dark parking lot biding them a safe journey home. After that day it was rare for her to see him, but on the other hand he saw her often. Studying her every move, no longer under my command, Janice continued to flourish, keeping her eyes on the prize, never noticing Thomas' existing presence. Until one night after leaving bible study heading home, trouble found a way to interrupt her life.

Brenda M. Files

Watching as she drove off waving goodnight to church members, he began to feel deep satisfaction. Having planned his evening to include Janice; shortly before the dismissal of service, Thomas, lurked in the shadows of a cold, moonless night outside the church while listening to the powerful, spirit filled praise and worship; engulfed in thoughts of wickedness. Tampering with Janice car, cutting a gash in the gas line, he allowed the fluids from the vehicle to escape and fall onto the ground. The smell of gas began to alert all members approaching the parking lot with overwhelming alarm brought on by the loudness of the odor, each promising in the stillness of the night, to report the matter to the gas company as soon as possible.

Being one of the last to leave the lot, Linda had only traveled a very short distance from help when her vehicle suddenly sputtered; coming to a complete stop. Fear immediately became a friend as the darkness yielded no long distant view on the blacken stretch of road, due to absent streetlamps. With the loud screams of crickets and other creeping things in the background sounding their nightly alarms, her heart raced rapidly, she suddenly saw headlights vastly approaching, while looking through her rear view mirror.

Giving God praise for sending a ram in the bush, during her time of trouble; little did she know, it was not a ram, but a raging bull, with sharp piercing horns, aimed straight for his unsuspecting victim. Noticing the car slowing its speed, Janice became excited by the fact; help had arrived. She became increasingly happy once the driver exited his car, and the tall figure was dressed in a top ranking uniform, one she knew all too well. A few seconds later the unknown body finally came into perfect view, she recognized the person standing next to her car window.

Thankful for the surprise, Janice rolled down the pane of glass saluting while announcing, "Am I glad to see you General! As you can tell, I've found myself in a very precarious situation."

"Well young lady, what seems to be the problem?" He deliberately asked, but already knew.

"To tell you the truth, I have no idea. The car was working fine before arriving for church, but after leaving, heading home, without warning it just died."

Seemingly very concerned, he suggested, "Let me turn my car around so it will face yours, that way I can check under the hood with assistance from my headlights. First, let me be clear, I don't know much about small engines, but maybe I can help find the solution." Without question, she welcomed the helping hand extended. With the cars facing each other, headlights shining brightly in her face, she swiftly placed her hands in front of her eyes to shield them from the high beams blinding her view.

Purposely creating the situation, Thomas got out of his car, walked over, once again making a suggestion, "sorry, but since it is so dark on this isolated stretch of road, not to mention spooky, we will need all the light my car can transmit, and probably a knowledgeable mechanic in the end. In the meantime, have a seat in my car and I'll take a look under your hood."

Eager to cooperate, she gave no hesitation in conforming to the proposal. Taking a seat on the passenger side of the car, she watched his every move as he checked the engine. Shortly thereafter, walking around the vehicle to get inside her car, he sat under the stirring wheel, pretending to make efforts in starting the motor.

Moments later, Thomas walked slowly over to the car where Janice was sitting, wiping his hands on a large white

Brenda M. Files

handkerchief to announce his diagnosis. Ready, and waiting to hear some positive news, welcoming his, or any opinion, she listened closely to every word spoken.

"Well young lady, from what I can see, but more so what can be smelled; the problem may be a possible gas leak, or something of that nature."

Covering her mouth in shock for a few seconds, she soon stated, "when we were leaving the church, a group of us smelled gas, but quickly agreed that it was coming from somewhere in the surrounding area. We believed the loud odor was possibly a church problem, never suspecting the smell could be coming from beneath my car."

"Sorry to tell you this, but you'll have to get someone to tow it in, this car is hazardous; not suitable for driving."

"Just my luck," sounding annoyed,

"I lost my cell phone today, and I didn't have time to go purchase another one, because I didn't want to miss bible study, hopefully you have one I may use for a few moments."

"Sorry to disappoint you, but mine is at the office. If you would like, I can take you over to a friend's home who lives close by. I'm sure she will allow you the use of her telephone, and wait for a tow truck to arrive. Would you like that?"

Responding without thought, "Yes! Yes, I would love it, but only if you, or your friend don't mind the intrusion."

"It would be our pleasure. Besides, I can't leave a damsel in distress."

"Thank you so much General!"

"No thanks necessary. Like I said, it will be a pleasure."

After locking up the vehicle, getting back inside his car, they drove down the long, cold, dark road...together.

Less than ten minutes later, they pulled into a very up scale, suburban community, stopping in front of a large two story, French Tutor style home; a home Janice could only dream of owning one day, she began inquiring, "Is this the home of your friend?"

Dismissing her question, he responded, "Please....get out of the car, and come with me." Doing as requested, she followed closely behind him. Ringing the doorbell, Thomas waited with wicked thoughts, for someone to answer; looking at Janice with a broad smile on his face. Seemingly growing impatient behind the long delay in answering, Thomas decided to knock vigorously on the door; gathering the attention of the person he knew was inside.

After the second knock, the door swung open; standing there was another familiar face she had seen on base, a face belonging to, Brigadier General Kandi Douglas, dressed in a thin night gown, matching robe and shoes: even lounging she was elegant. Hesitantly Kandi opened her home with a fake cheer of politeness, to the unwelcomed female.

After the greetings, and applauding compliments had been attributed to the beauty of her home, decorated in a breath taking traditional style, before another word could be said, Thomas took control.

"Sorry we came by without calling, but I found Janice stranded on the side of the road with a broken car. I tried to assist in getting it started again, but the job was too difficult for my limited capabilities. With neither of us having our cell phones, I thought you would help out our stranded motorist, and fellow soldier, by allowing her the use your telephone while waiting here for a tow truck."

Annoyed by the female presence, but not the man she loves, Kandi guided the young woman to where she could have privacy, giving permission to use the telephone.

Brenda M. Files

Returning to the room, looking around trying to locate Thomas, who was nowhere to be found, but a few seconds later walked through the front door; prompting Kandi to ask him in a whisper, "Why did you bring her here? Do you think the same thing is going to happen again.......in my house?"

"Why not in your house? I thought what you and I have, is ours, we're a team."

"Tell me, how do you propose the team pull this off? Don't forget, she is calling a towing service, which means she is giving them her name, and my address as her pick up location."

Before he could answer, they were interrupted by Janice's announcement, "Sorry to barge in on your conversation, but the telephone isn't working."

Glancing over at Thomas for a moment, knowing he had something to do with the pause in her service; Kandi returned her sight back toward Janice, replying. "That's funny, the phone was working fine earlier this afternoon. Sorry, but I don't own a cell phone, can't stand them; they leave you with no freedom!"

Realizing what he had done, but unknown to Janice, Thomas had secretly gone outside, and cut the phone wires during the time they left the room. After the bad news was shared concerning no working communication devices, Thomas pretending to be helpful said, "Let me check to see what could have possibly happened."

While the phone lines were being checked, Kandi offered the guest a place to sit, and something to drink; her hospitality was accepted. Leaving Janice alone, Kandi went to prepare glasses of wines from the bottle gifted to her by their last victim. Soon returning with the beverages in tow, Thomas entering behind her broadcasted more bad news.

Saluting Madness   83

"I know you don't want to hear this Janice, but apparently the phone lines are down; hopefully they will be working again shortly. This happens all the time around here, but before we know it, lines were quickly operational again. We'll just have to keep checking; I'm quite sure you want to get home. In the meantime, we'll make you as comfortable as possible: at least until we can get a tow truck out here to rescue you."

"I have already been rescued, saved from a dark, lonesome road that could have been very dangerous for me. For this I raise my glass in appreciation!" Everyone lifted their stemware, clanging them together in acceptance of the kind word spoken by their unsuspecting guest.

Slowly, the extra ingredient Thomas added to her glass of wine, once he came back inside, started to have an effect on her. Becoming aware her words were slurring, and the capability of focusing difficult, Janice rang out, "something is wrong! I feel strangely lightheaded."

Trying to stand up, she collapsed back down into the chair; hurriedly Thomas sprung into action, gathering the young lady into his arms, carrying the limp, unaware body of their next victim into their chamber of wickedness, the place where they found pleasure, sexually abusing women.

The next morning she found herself in her apartment, on her bed, fully dressed in the same clothes from the day before, dazed and confused. Unsure of what happened during the previous evening shared with officers, she grew sad. Finally coming into focus as the bright morning light, streamed through her window, she glanced over and looked at the clock; realizing the lateness of the hour Janice picked up the telephone, and called her command station. Without reprimand she was given the opportunity to know all was

Brenda M. Files

well, because it was well known, tardiness has never been a part of her work ethic.

Getting out of bed, dressing with some difficulty, and still in a groggy state of mind, she found discomfort, and soreness on her thighs and vaginal area, also noticing a few marks of bodily bruising, she knew advantages had been taken, but she couldn't remember a thing. Once she arrived on base; exiting the cab hired to bring her to work, the first face she saw was Kandi, greeting and saluting in a cheerful outcry. "How are you doing today? Are you okay? We were worried about you when we realized you were heavily intoxicated, unable to properly function without assistance. Finally we were able to take you home, after searching your purse to find an address."

Trying not to look confused, or bewilder, because of memory loss, Janice stated, "I'm okay, just surprised I overslept, now late for work. However, I would like to extend once again, my thanks to both of you for helping me last night, I'm truly grateful."

"You're so welcome, and I will certainly relay your sentiments to Thomas! By the way....did you get in touch with a tow truck company?"

"I have plans on doing that first thing today, I was too exhausted to complete that mission last night."

"Well, I wish you the best of luck, getting all of that straighten out. Take care of yourself." Satisfied with Janice's pleasing demeanor, and responses, Kandi saluted, and dismissed the young soldier, ending all conversations, disappearing completely from one another's company.

However, as Janice walked away she was not convinced that all was well after spending an evening in the home of a superior officer, but lacked evidence to support, or prove suspicions of sinister acts possibly done to her.

Nevertheless, before leaving home for work that morning, she did something truly disgusting in her mind, and to her body, she didn't shower before getting dressed. Feeling guilty about being late for work, about an hour later she requested the rest of the day off; once okayed she hastily proceeded to a medical facility off base. Upon the completion of the physical exam, all tests results back; disappointingly the doctor relayed to Janice, not only did her vaginal area show trauma, and abrasion consistent with rape, the blood work confirmed she had been administered drugs. Pleased that all of her suspicions had been curtailed, replaced with truth about her commanders, she developed feelings of disgust and shame.

Even with the doctors information as proof of being assaulted; she knew it would be a difficult road to bring them down as her assailants; she grew hopelessness numb. Suddenly, Janice started to believe this couldn't be their first time, leading her to pursue justice against the two until the bitter end, refusing to be intimidated, or end her career as a soldier.

Unfortunately, after a lengthy personal investigation, she found no one to corroborate her belief, not even a tow truck driver, or a church member lagging behind on that long, dark road. However, two things were proven, the gas line had been tampered with, and the car had been located where she said it would be found. A year later, with advancements, and very hard work, she transferred from the base of horror, headed for a new destination with greater opportunities awaiting."

After reading only a these mind blowing tragedies of senseless rapes, including the handy work of my mother; emptiness took the place of love for the lady I use to believe was my mother. At this point I began to agree with

Brenda M. Files

my father's warning, and did not view the recorded videos of these horrific displays. Suddenly I became nauseated: quickly getting up from the hospital chair, running into the restroom, only to miss by quite a few inches, my oval target. Having made an unsightly mess; not wanting housekeeping to see the disgusting art work, I started the gruesome task of cleaning vomit off the walls, floors, and seat of the commode; struggling to recover from raging intestines.

Even when the cleaning of the unpleasant disastrous, fowl odor was complete, my system seemed to still be against me. Retrieving a face cloth from the towel rack, soaking it with cold water and placing the compress against my forehead, a half hour later my stomach started to calm, helping my mind to relax from the soul consuming information. Nevertheless, I had to continue reading.

"As you now know all too well, his brother Grant, and his family have been subjected to Thomas controlling, manipulation for years, but the saddest part is the willingness of your mother getting involved in these methodical, evil ways. Kandi has left everyone who has learned of her actions with a large question mark, about the character of the woman we thought we knew. I was never really around Grant, or his wife to get a real feel of them as individuals, but they seemed to be good for each other, nice people loving their children; would do anything to protect them.

Needless to say, at some point down the road, Thomas brought Kandi into his world as a partner to continue the assault on his niece, Amy. Agreeing to remain silent during each filming of his sexual encounter against the young child, your mother became physically acquainted with her the day after her fifteenth birthday. Late one evening

Thomas phoned requesting Kandi's presence at a seedy motel found just off highway ninety-eight, a place where the two had visited before. Meeting on the outside of the rented room where cloudy skies began to release large drops of rain, he introduced her to the instructions of what was to be expected; like a good little child charmed by the hissing sound exiting his snake like tongue, she listened to every word of his diabolical plan. Entering the motel room, she laid eyes on an incoherent child lying on the bed disrobed, wearing nothing but her smooth, flawless skin, and a blindfold, swaying slightly from side to side, struggling to be freed from the bondage of imprisonment. Meanwhile, Kandi began remembering the first time she was included in his misguided, trifecta interlude; found the discomfort she felt then was the same once again. In fierce efforts, she tried to discuss the situation with Thomas, but her words fell on death ears. Regrettably nothing, or no one seemed to matter to Thomas when it came to pleasing himself, especially not Kandi. Knowing she would never stop being on board, because of the deep love she carried for him, his disrespect continued to gain solid ground for her, and unfortunately she remained a willing participant.

When all was over between the three of them, most of the sexual act he made your mother perform on the victim, and vice-a-versa, but never would she refute the climactic pleasure obtained, during their unspeakable, deviant behavior. As time marched on, Thomas would bring the blindfold teenager into the privacy of Kandi's home for their pleasure. At first your mother blew a gasket, but time mellowed all of her reservations and unpleasant thoughts; finding much solace in knowing what was to come from their young, drug induced star.

Brenda M. Files

CHAPTER EIGHT

Sometime son I wonder who in the world did I fall in love, marry, and produce my beautiful children with? Regardless of these questions, one thing I do know, all of you are special creations from God above, but my love was not enough to protect you all from the flood of disasters that was vastly approaching, heading straight into our lives. It was a tidal wave, no one could have foreseen or prepare for. A couple of years after my transition back into civilian life, I left all the worries of the military, Thomas and your mother behind me, but in the end this would only be wishful thinking. After inheriting the contents of these explosive, nitroglycerin filled pages, my world was blasted, shattered into a million pieces.

Regrettably, because of my cowardly absence, Trinity learned of the many treacherous acts of Thomas through a very hard lesson in life, an act no one should ever endure.

However, I want you to know, your mother had no knowledge at first, about this ultimate betrayal against our child, but your sister had been and still is, mentally and physically scared. I only discovered this brutal attack when Thomas graphic details were placed before me, disclosing his vicious crimes.

Immediately after learning these evil deed, I came home to be with, and stand by Trinity's side. Hesitantly she allowed me into her collapsed world, a world believed to be forever disgraced. Although it took a week before she felt comfortable enough to truly confide in me the full details of the horrific saga, it made me sick; so sick I wanted to once again, kill Thomas.

Living in her mother's home at the time, Thomas knew she would be alone, because everyone was away for the weekend. A junior at the university, just finishing her final exams, she planned for a quiet evening at home, a long hot bath, a unhealthy meal of junk food, and a relaxing, mindless evening in front of the television.

Filling the tub with water, relishing the moment her toes would feel the sensation from the warm water, she walked around the house in the manner she loved, naked. Enjoying the freedom of her nudity, the sweet thoughts of no tests, or classes; little did Trinity know, Thomas had made copies of keys stolen from Kandi for future entrances into their home. These were keys Kandi never wanted to share with him; lacking trust in his unstable ways. Turning on some music, pouring a large glass of red wine, lighting a few scented candles, placing them around the outside perimeter of the bathtub, she stepped into a sanctuary of escape; gliding slowly into her piece of heaven on earth.

Relaxing deeply within the fragrant water, a bountiful amount of suds climbing up her body, gently caressing the bottom of her chin; alerting her eyes to close as her mind received peaceful solitude. A short while later without warning, a strange, but familiar voice rang out in the background, giving great startle to the unaware young lady. Ready to scream, when the hand of Thomas covered her mouth, silencing any utterance parting from her lips: boldly stating, "If you want to live another day, do not make a sound...understand!" With these words spoken through clinched teeth, a knife pressed against her chest, she nodded yes. Slowly he removed his hand from her mouth saying, "remember, you promised not to yell, but if you do, make sure you're ready for the consequences." Terrified she followed every word of his instructions.

Demanding her out of the bathtub, Trinity slowly rose from the water with a vast amount of soapsuds richly

Brenda M. Files

covering her glowing skin of bronze, while trembling feverously. Extending her hand downward to pick up the extra large, plush towel resting on the side of the tub, to cover her nude body, she was quickly denied the privilege. Grabbing the towel, throwing it across the room, removing it from her reach, Thomas raised the volume of his voice, giving orders once again. "Get out of the tub! And don't worry about the dripping water from your body, its only leaving a clean trail to our new beginning." Astonished, Trinity continued to say nothing, not because she had a loss for words, but fearing what was not known as the crazed person continued speaking his demands, "now I want you to dance toward me very slowly!"

Again she followed his instructions, while leaving a trail of soapsuds, during her dance performance.

Time seemed to move slowly for my daughter as the host of horror led her into a day of living hell. Pleading in fear as she was escorted into the bedroom, "Mr. Thomas, please change your mind about anything you're planning."

"I just want to spend a little time with you. I hope you want to spend time with me too."

"I would sir if my mother was home, but without her being present, and me being undressed, she would not approve of the time we are sharing alone." Annoyed with the response he screamed, "your mother ask me to check in, keep a watchful eye on you, so I'm doing exactly what I promised I would do! I'm going to keep my eyes on that lovely body you possess!"

"Sir, I don't think this is what she had in mind for you to do."

"Regardless....this is what I have in mind for me to do for you. Now if you don't mind, let's end any discussions concerning Kandi, and what she want!"

Disappointed by her lack of persuasion, she decided on trying to guide all his thoughts toward being good friends with our family.

"Mr. Thomas, you know how much, and how long my parents have loved you and your family, so you should know how much this will hurt them if they found out you brought harm to their daughter."

"That is why they will not find out! You see, I know your parents were married, breaking military codes since their careers began. Now, if you keep our secret close to your heart, I will keep their secret close to mine, unless, you want your mother to be disgraced by court martial, receive an dishonorable discharge, and Charles retirement revoked. Now tell me, do we tell secrets, or should I walk out of this house, make a report about their infractions to the oversight committee, or stay here and we have fun together? Your choice, your decision!"

Becoming frozen in her thoughts, Trinity's body movements increased in aggressive trembles, not only from fear, but also being wet, disrobed and cold. A long pause ensued, when she heard him ask, "are you going to be a good girl?" with no recourse she nodded, yes. Having never been with a man before, guilt bound her to a blinding anguish, while suggesting in a child like voice, "whatever you're going to do Mr. Thomas, do not do anything in my mother's bedroom, this would be totally disrespectful." Enjoying the control; the painful look in her eyes, he came over to where she stood, almost nose to nose, grabbed the triceps of her arms, pulled their bodies together and placed his mouth over hers, forcing an unwanted kiss.

Struggling to push away from his aggressive embrace, he gave a reminder in a stern tone, "If you fight, your parents loose." Immediately, her lips receive the unwanted

Brenda M. Files

invitation of being bathe in the sinful, moisture of his mouth; allowing his slithering tongue to dance toward the back of her throat.

Once released from his firm hold, silently Trinity continued to tremble out of control standing in the center of the bedroom floor, forcefully watching him undress. A few moments later, completely exposed, he led her by the hand to lie down on the bed to begin his ownership of a body, no longer declared as hers. Minutes turned into hours, hours turned into days; folding in long nights of abusive rape. The only time he allowed her out of the bedroom, were times they went into the kitchen to prepare something eat, or use the bathroom. He never allowed her to do anything alone, demanding all doors to remain opened at all times for his derange viewing; adding to her humiliation.

Early on the third morning, unable to sleep, Trinity was very happy when Thomas said as he closely watched her prepare breakfast, sounding more, and more like a narcissistic maniac, "Well Trinity, my love, our time has been great, but these beautiful moments of peaceful bliss must come to a close, because the family is due to return sometime today and we don't want them to find us here together, do we? This would cause much scandal if anyone learned you and I have been involved in an affair behind your mother's back; a woman who loves me totally. She is someone I'd hate to test her love concerning the two of us, wouldn't you?" displaying a sinister grin.

Looking at him with contempt, she replied truthfully, "Only if I'm afraid of the response. Mr. Thomas, I believe in my mother, just like she believes in, and loves me. So no, I wouldn't have any concerns for her love being tested. How about you?" Releasing her statements no longer in fear, but strong surges of confidence; deliberately Thomas never answered the purposed question.

After breakfast they went into the living room, where he placed her on the floor and assaulted her once again, this time more aggressively than the first. Finally completing his journey inside of her innocent womb, he announced, "You may now take a shower." Before he could complete the sentence, she leaped from the floor, started walking briskly toward the bathroom, when suddenly she heard him say in a thunderous voice, "BUT!!" Stopping, but refusing to turn around, she stood there waiting for whatever came next. "The rules still apply...I will watch your every move. I also want you to cleanse me first, then I will participate in cleaning you from head to toe; agreed?" Consumed with total disgust, she innocently replied, "Agreed."

Once they had cleansed themselves, Trinity quickly put on a large sweat suit, thick socks and fuzzy slippers in effort to get warm, but also heavily cover her body from continued observation by a crazed maniac. In the meantime, after putting his clothes on, he walked toward the door, causing Trinity to become extremely giddy throughout her entire body; watching his backside grow further away from where she stood. Suddenly stopping, he turned around; anxiety overwhelmed her thoughts, ears began to pound as if someone had entered her head without permission, playing a drum set, striking cymbals loudly, but never once did she stop listening to his words,

"Always remember family, what it will take to keep them from danger, and a whole lot of shame. You will keep all secrets sealed behind closed lips, or family is no longer safe," stating this while planting a finger over his lips. A few seconds later he turned, walk out the house, closing the door behind him. Without delay Trinity ran to the door,

Brenda M. Files

turning each lock to its secured position, including the safety chain. With her mission completed, she laid against the large frame of wood, weeping profusely. After that day Trinity was never the same, soon moving out of her mother's home.

A week later sounding distraught, she called asking me to come home; I caught the first flight available, to be with my troubled daughter. After arriving at her place, she answered the door, let me inside, leaped into my arms, held on tightly, while I vowed never to allow hurt to overtake her again. Removing her grasp from around my neck, looking into my eyes, she blurted out, "I have something bad to tell you daddy! Thomas came over here last night, but thinking it was family, I opened the door allowing him to force his way inside to rape me again! How does he find me daddy! I am so sorry! I am so sorry!" she cried aloud. With both of us broken, I finally said, "you have nothing to be sorry for my beautiful child. Always remember, I'm with you no matter what, but right now sweetie, I hate to put you through this; we need to call the police, also tell your mother about what happened. I know this may seem hard, but once we do this you will feel so much better. Right now, I'm taking you to the hospital, afterwards I will ask your mother to meet us at her home, because of a family emergency."

Still sobbing, Trinity tried to gather her composure; struggling, she said, "telling her it is an emergency will cause her to become reckless."

"To late, she has been reckless for a long time. Her recklessness is the reason I am here consoling my daughter. Your mother should have had control over her home before extending rights to Thomas, allowing him access to you. So let her behind panic, let her continue in recklessness, I really don't care."

"What if she is blinded by horrible thoughts, become involved in a car accident and get hurt? I couldn't handle that daddy, because it would be my fault."

"Well, to keep you from worrying about your mother, or a possible accident, I'll just say you have something to discuss with the both of us, and need to talk while you still having the nerves, she'll automatically think pregnant. Therefore, she will be herself, and you'll be happy, okay."

"Okay," she sadly replied.

Once we left the hospital and filed a police report, I made the phone call and we immediately went to Kandi's home. Still having a key, Trinity opened the door, allowing us access; her mother had not yet arrived. Growing frighten, Trinity paced back, and forth across the floor. About ten minutes later, we could hear the tumblers of the deadbolts sounding its alarm that keys were unlocking the door, and trouble was coming inside.

A few seconds later the door opened; slamming closed in almost the same instance, followed by loud sounds of claps escaping from the bottom of Kandi's shoes onto the hardwood flooring. The thunderous sounds granted me the satisfaction of knowing how easily her mind could be lead to think of herself, and not her daughter's well being. In the next instance, her voice yelled out in detectable anger, "Trinity where are you?!"

Shortly thereafter, her search found us sitting in the den where we had been patiently waiting for her arrival. However, I had changed my mind about being beside her, and allowed Trinity to sit on the sofa alone so she could have independence, and not lean on me as a crutch, but if needed, I'd be by her side in a flash. Looking across the

Brenda M. Files

room with a large question mark written all over her face, Kandi walked toward our daughter without the hint of a smile, asking in a calm tone; trying not to become unraveled, "Are you okay?" This time, without the elevated volume of shoes assisting in her approach, she extended her hands, pulled Trinity up to stand so they could embrace each other, and once again ask in a tone of pretense, "Are you okay? Are you hurt?" Immediately the tears from Trinity's eyes gave way for the uncontrollable water works to flow freely. Surprised by the soothing comfort of motherly concern, a feeling she truly needed, gave her a peace of mind; a great belief in her mother. I knew better.

After a few moments Kandi stated, "calm down; tell me what's bothering you." Shaking for a few seconds longer, Trinity found the capability of locating her voice, "I have something to tell you, I have been wanting to do so for a long time, but was to afraid." Slightly agitated by what seemed to be a childish behavior, especially since her thought were still being applied to pregnancy, she replied, "stop being upset, just tell me what's going on." Looking around the room to locate my eyes for reassurance, Trinity began to speak clearly. "Mother please have a seat next to me; this conversation will take more than a moment to discuss." Filled with suspense Kandi found her place on the sofa; Trinity moved over to sit closer; for security.

Clutching her mother's hands, she hurriedly began spitting out the bitter pills of ugly details. "I know it's been a very long road to travel with me, while acting strangely toward my family, losing many friends, not wanting to complete my education, not because of anything you two have done, or anything I did, except for not opening up my mouth to tell someone what happened; withdrawal and silence came forth because of shame, fear and threats."

Saluting Madness   97

Desiring desperately to know about the person who impregnated her daughter, fury rose greatly inside of Kandi, but without interruption she continued to listen. However, what she heard next made the hair on the nape of her neck stand up straight, and her head pound, "I was raped!" Weeping, she repeated the same three words in a loud voice, over, and over again. "I was rape! I was raped! I was raped! I was raped!"

At this juncture, I jumped up, went over to the sofa, sat down, gathered her in my arms, rocked her back, and forth like she was a baby; her mother's face became covered with tears. Time permitted each of us to gather our composure, retrieve tissue from the bathroom to absorb the flow of water, and relieve clogged nostrils.

Later, Trinity turned, looking deep into her mother's eyes, continuing to expose the ugly truth that would not end well, "I was raped over an entire weekend when you, and the rest of the family were away visiting grandmother. I thought I was living in hell on earth. I saw Satan close up! Last night, the satanic rapist came, and attacked me again!"

After filling her mother in, Trinity delivered the final blow that would make, or break their relationship.

"Mother," she nervously stated, but immediately took a couple of seconds to pause for a breathing session before continuing. "I have not wanted to utter this name since these horrible encounters happened, but because of disgust, not only do I want to say the name, but need to say it! I want to say the name, not only for my sanity, but to also reveal his ugly, insane nature."

"You just tell us and we, your parents will help find justice for this heinous crime. As a matter of fact, with the way I'm feeling I may find a way to kill him myself." Enthused by the support, willingly she held Kandi's hands tightly inside hers, often glancing at me for trusting smiles. Gently she nodded her head as if she was telling me, 'I can do this,' then turned to look again into her mother's eyes. Without blinking she blurted out the name she wanted to forget, "It was Mr. Thomas! It was General Thomas Laskey who raped me!" Immediately Kandi snatched her hand from the inside our daughter's, stood up, and walked across the room. Desponded, she stood silently with her back turned for a great length of time, leading us to follow her lead in silence. Having private thoughts for awhile, she finally turned around to face us once again saying, "I just can't believe Thomas would do such a thing!" sounding displeased, disappointed, and upset by his behavior.

Quickly joining forces alongside Kandi, I did not speak on what my thoughts had been, instead saying, "I'm in agreement with whatever you ladies decide to do to get justice, the consequences doesn't matter. This includes losing earthly things we've always thought were important to us, but the important things now is to protect, and care for the gifts God gave to us, our children. Now ladies, what are we going to do?" Without reluctance, Trinity replied, "have him prosecuted!"

Silence from Kandi spoke volumes; commanding our attentions. Gazing at my innocent, precious daughter shaking from the fear of the unknown, she calmly waited for Kandi to say something. Unfortunately I was not willing to break for intermission, time out, or station identification. Angrily, I roared dislike for her deliberate disdain. This time I walked and approached swiftly to where she was standing; nose to nose, releasing piercing words and a vast amount of moisture from my mouth onto her face, daring the frighten lady to move, or not listen to what I had to say.

"What is wrong with you woman? Have you lost your mind, and soul completely?! Your daughter is crying out for your help, and all she can get is nothing! You should be ashamed of yourself! If not, I'm ashamed of you, and for you! Although, while looking at you, I realize you may be just as crazy as Thomas; lying in the same swamp of madness, right by his side?!"

Suddenly realizing this entire situation was not about me, or Kandi, but the young lady who is my child; looking withdrawn by our behavior.

Feeling badly, because I had lost control, I surrendered to shame; allowing embarrassment to escort me to covering my lips, and blanket me in humiliation.

Seeing the response of covering my mouth, Trinity gave me comfort, "thanks dad for your caring love." Offended by mine and Trinity's response, Kandi lashed out at the both of us. "No one wants me to be happy! I don't understand why you all can't see that Thomas is really making me happy! Charles, instead of you brainwashing our children into believing lies, inducing them to create false allegations, because of your jealousy, you should teach them about love. You've caused them to be ashamed as children, now you have placed them in a situation to bring more shame."

Remaining calm while withstanding the voice of ignorance, I reframed from comment, allowing stupidity to continue. Surprisingly, Trinity brought forth angry artillery of her own; putting on her armor of defense, she sounded off in displeasure. "My father has never brought us shame; standing here today he has only made me proud. You on the other hand should be very ashamed, because I didn't do anything wrong! Aren't you doing something wrong, by not standing with me? Aren't you causing yourself shame?"

Brenda M. Files

Given no opportunity to answer, Trinity continued reprimanding her mother.

"Since you're policing, and criticizing dad's actions in this battle, a war that has nothing to do with him, or his past, except the fact that I am his child, please allow me to remind you that this has everything to do with the monster you brought into our lives, and you having no concerns for my feelings, or the truth! The truth is, I had to endure rape for your happiness, not once, but twice, now you have the audacity to say, I've become brainwashed! I would not allow anyone to create, or make me tell an pernicious lie such as rape! I wouldn't do this to anyone, especially a well decorate general just to fulfill my father's agenda! You must be losing your mind! Most of all, my father would not waste his precious time to get even because of jealousy, against a deranged person like Thomas! If you believe this, then dad is right, you're just as crazy as he is. I pray God will have mercy on your soul, but as for me, I will no longer have faith, or trust in you as a mother, ever again!"

By this time, Trinity's face was drenched in tears, but held strong in her voice of power. Kandi responding forcefully, "I am you mother! I wish you wouldn't open doors for such heartless remarks to enter in, not to mention thoughtless insults hurdled toward..," before another word could escape Kandi's mouth, she was interrupted in mid sentence. "I wish you hadn't laid out a platform that extended an invitation for heartless remarks, or room for thoughtless insults could be hurdled toward you.

"How dare you continue to speak to your mother in such a ugly manner?!"

"How dare you not hold your raped daughter in your arms?! How dare you not denounce future involvement, or contact with Thomas, never to speak his name again, except at the police station standing next to me?"

Silence once again took control of the room. After the quiet continued to consume the house, Trinity grabbed her purse off the sofa, stared at her mother for a few moments, then turn and walked out the house, just after slamming Kandi's door keys on the table. Shortly thereafter, I followed behind her, but not before taking all covers from my mouth.

"I hope you are truly happy, and if you are able to live a long, fulfilling life with a rapist, I agree with Trinity, may God have mercy on your soul. But as for me and my child, we no longer have faith, or trust in you as a person, or mother. Believe it or not, I am not jealous, nor do I hate you; as a matter of fact I have no thoughts, or feelings other than pity for you. Good bye Kandi, take care of yourself."

"But Nella...." calling me by my middle name, a name lovingly used when trying to control, my heart. However, on that note I walked out of her home, deciding the only way I would look in the direction of my ex wife again, was in support of Trinity, standing beside our daughter at the police station, bringing formal charges against Thomas, or at his trial after he's found guilty; led away in handcuffs.

Since that day, Trinity has not spoken to her mother.

After learning of this horrible dysfunctional situation of grand proportion, I readily decided to move from the place that was clearly dear to me, (my hometown) to be near my children. I also accepted an offer to become the pastor of a small church centrally located, near my family.

However, I had a great amount of reservation about being near Kandi and Thomas, not because of possibly losing everything I had worked hard for, or being harmed physically; instead, what I may do to them.

Shortly after arriving back in a city I loathed, Trinity moved in with me until we could find her a better place to live, other than her small studio apartment. Meanwhile, we began seeking out professional counseling for her, so my child could have a better chance for a stable future.

Once we moved Trinity into her new place, later that same day, we found ourselves sitting on the floor in front of the fireplace wrapped in cozy blankets, listening to the crackling of the wood as it burned and flicker light in the darken room, while drinking a hot cup of cocoa. As I sat next to my daughter, with her head lying on my shoulder, we listened to the music of the fire's snapping crisp sound, and the volume of muted echoes in the room; extended me the opportunity to share with her the history of Thomas, how he gained such great power over our family, and why I seemed so powerless. But unfortunately this madman had already shared these ugly things with her in great details."

Finishing the reading of draining documents for the time being, closing the ugly pages of my family's directed life, I looked across the room at my father and began smiling, because the understanding as to why my sister had withdrawn and became a recluse; was now finally clear.

CHAPTER NINE

Time seemed to continue its life without any signs of regret, repercussions, or consequences brought against Thomas, a man still controlling other people lives. The road of justice never seemed willing to give a flicker of light in our direction, but little did our family know, a flicker would soon yield a spark, creating a flame that would bring storm of hell's fire and brimstone. This production would circle around Thomas, engulfing his sinister ways as if they were sheets of paper consumed by hot, molting lava.

Junior, there is something you don't know on a personal level about the Laskey's......they had five children instead of two. They had three sons, and two daughters, not to include Diamond, and Terrance. Thomas was hard on the boys, causing Peggy to always remind him they were not soldiers in the military, but beloved children of their household. He often gave difficult demands, releasing foul words and showing them little attention; treating the girls like princesses. This blatant show of difference, caused great hardship, making Peggy struggles difficult to keep their children grounded; constantly reassuring her son's the only difference between them was age, dates of birth, and gender. During the course of these ongoing battles of keeping peace, Peggy found herself in the middle of a civil war in the mist of her own home. In the end there would be no winners, when her sons were sent away to live in other homes. Peggy hated Thomas for this selfish act, but decided to stay with him to make her marriage work. Her sons never forgave her for not standing with them, and she never forgave herself. Those young men never saw their parents again, nor did they want too.

Brenda M. Files

Meanwhile, as seasons changed, time soon changed Taylor, the oldest daughter of the Laskey's. Maturing into a very voluptuous young lady, she began rebelling against her controlling father's, insisting on using her own mind; building a brick wall against whatever he stood for.

Son, after seeing you today, later in the evening I went out to grab a bite to eat; returning home I found Taylor, a scared young lady, sitting in the dark, crouched on my front steps waiting for me; her face lathered in tears. Rushing up the sidewalk to extend comfort, I sat down, placed my arm around her shoulders, but was immediately rejected as she looked; searching recognition. Once she located clarity, my chest was used for her bed of comfort. Gathering myself from the steps, pulling her up by the hand to stand alongside me, I guided the tear blinded young lady inside the house, led her to the sofa in the den, hurriedly sat next to her and placed my arm around her shoulder; readying myself to listen to whatever was troubling the young lady.

"Mr. Malloy, I have been in a living hell most of my life, at least what I can, or want to remember." Pausing for a few seconds, she wiped her face, and beneath her nose with the sleeve on her forearm, then released a long, slow sigh before continuing. "I'm sorry to intrude on your private time, but having no idea where to go, or who to trust, without much thought you came to mind. You have always listened to me when I was angry, happy or sad, never judging, or giving a lecture for any of my behaviors. That's why I believe, I can tell you anything without worry of hearing it again, but if you don't want to hear these troubles there won't be any hard feelings about your decision." Deciding not to say anything, I extended a smile, allowing her all the room she needed to express herself.

"Growing up in our home as a little girl, everyone thought my sister, and I were special when we went to work with our father, treating us like royalty, particularly you. Always inviting us into your office, allowing us to take turns to spin around in your chair, the chair you needed to sit and finish your work. You always had a smile and a piece of candy to share with us. We were happy children, we were fairy princesses. However, one morning while getting ready for school I became ill, running a low grade fever, causing my parents to make the decision of not allowing me to attend school, but sending me back to bed. Staying home with my mom so she could take care of me, I became even more excited it was Friday; thanking God for allowing me the luxury of a long, unexpected weekend. My mother was always the best at making us feel better with the warmth of her love: it didn't hurt I had her all to myself for the day.

Later, around lunchtime, dad came home to check in on us, making sure I didn't need to see the doctor.

Upon his arrival when he walked through the door, mommie looked surprised, but   seemed very excited by his presence, exclaiming, "I didn't know you were coming home for lunch! If I had, there would have been something prepared for your lunch."

"I didn't come home to have lunch, I've already eaten, just wanted to check in on my little angel; making sure she was doing okay."

After walking across the room, and sitting down on the sofa, where she had allowed me to come to rest so I would be closer to her as she worked downstairs; he rubbed my forehead, searching for a sign of continued fever; while giving me a smile, and a wink. At the same time, mommie was standing in the background watching very lovingly, the

　　　　　　　　　　　　　　　Brenda M. Files

gentle attentiveness dad gave, smiling at his movements of concern.

Finally she said, "well I'm glad you decided to come home, I need to go and pick up a couple of things from the grocery store for dinner. I didn't want to leave Taylor here alone, so if you don't mind, will you stick around for a while; possibly prepare her some lunch?" "Mind! It would be my pleasure to stay here with my angel. You just go, and take your time. Remember, I'm the boss on the base, so I can take as long as needed, especially when it comes down to the caring of my family." Smiling, listening to his beautiful words of love, gathering her purse, she made an exit.

Feeling a little better and wanting something to eat, I began rattling off my desires for a meal. A short while later, daddy returned with a tray, carrying everything my heart desired. Sitting down next to me as I began to eat my meal he gently stroked my hair. Having no thoughts other than how much I was loved by my parents, especially my father, but half way through the consumption of my lunch, I felt my dad's hand rubbing up, and down my back in a different manner. This was not the way usual, loving touches should feel; this touch caused me to feel very uncomfortable. I started to feel like the young girls my mother desperately tried to plant vividly in our head about the innocent being manipulated by a person preying upon innocent, unsuspecting victims, but I never saw the face of my father painted in the illustration of my mind. Trembling with fear, when he brushed my hair from my neck, kissing it, not as a father, but the predator I heard strongly announced in my mother's voice, while stressing danger. "Daddy," I lowly called out, "what are you doing?"

Dropping the half eaten sandwich onto the tray, missing the plate completely, he embraced me firmly in his arms. His next act caused me to lie my head against the back of my neck, swiftly moving it from side to side, trying to prevent my father from kissing my mouth; whispering, "be a good little girl for your daddy." Listening to his breathing as it became louder and heavier, I cried out loud, "Dad, please don't!"

"Do you know how much I love you? Do you know how far I would go to protect my girls from harm? That is why I need to know everything about you, not just outside, but also inwardly. I need to become familiar with you through the most private parts of you, because if someone tries to bring harm, I can seek them out like a hound. I need to have your scent planted firmly in my mind. I need you to become a bigger part of me," he stated while removing the tray from my lap. Pushing him by shoulder, trying to move his body and ugly intentions far away from me, but my strength was no match for his manly power. Forcing his hands on my legs, I repeated in an elevated voice,

"No daddy, you can't do this! I'm your daughter!"

No longer having the ability to hear me any longer; the man who was pawing me was no longer a father, but a man caring about his own feelings. A few seconds later, I felt his other hand traveling back, and forth across my back: whispering in a creepy, disturbing voice he said, "Daddy will not hurt his precious angel, so don't be frighten. All I want to do is teach you what true love really is, and how it should feel." Frighten I responded,

"but daddy," shaking with every word released, "I already know how much you love me. I know you, and mommie love me by the way you show it every day." Slowly, I could feel his half turned body, physical moving

108   Brenda M. Files

away from me. This caused me to grow in excitement, believing his mind had changed, and he would leave me alone; oh how wrong I was.

"Don't you bring your mother into this! Trust me, if I ever hear you are trying to stir up trouble by telling lies, I will forget that you are my daughter, and I'll have your mother's help. We'll have you committed into a institution for the insane; leaving you there forever! Know this, I can easily make everyone disappear whenever I get ready, so don't you dare try to cross me! do you understand?!"

Frighten into stiffness, the only thing left on my body capable of movement was my head; I nod yes.

Without words spoken, only a body piercing stare, he continued his gaze upon me, but thankfully the hand movement ceased. That was before he decided enough intimidation had been set in place, and proceeded rubbing me on different parts of my body.

Soon, he began moving his hand up, and down my thighs; moaning in growing, shameless pleasure. Using his other hand to guide my face toward his, ready to kiss my mouth, while warning me in loud voice of not biting him, or there would be regrets. With tears streaming down my face like a open faucet, I trembled like a leaf; helplessly being molested by my own father.

When my mother returned home, the sound of joy rang loudly from her voice as she closed the door behind her while carrying two bags of grocery, including the medicine the doctor had phoned in to the pharmacy for me, asking,

"How's our favorite patient doing? Did you check her temperature again, because I can see she didn't finish her lunch?" Frighten, I sunk deeper into the sofa, curled up and pulled the faux fur blanket tightly around my neck for the need of feeling protected, pretending to be asleep, and unaware of her return, but saw ever move she made.

Without a moment of delay in response, the stranger in our house replied, "she is doing just fine. She felt sleepy and drifted off quickly, so let's keep our voices down before we wake her." Although he knew I was awake, and had successfully instilled fear inside me, my eyes remained closed; never wanting to see him again. Later, all signs of fever had vanished, but I remained isolated from the family through a very long weekend, looking at the ceiling and four walls; leaving my room not even to eat.

After a couple of weeks of being in almost complete solitude, my mother had stress written all over her face, showing much concern for my well being, Chandler(my sister) cried often, pleading for me to talk to her. Daddy steered clear of my presence, until one afternoon after finally leaving, then arriving home from a long walk in the park, I found him alone, and it wasn't until the door had been closed and locked behind me, did I figure out there was no one in the house besides the two of us. Introduction to the same fear covering me on the day I was sick, causing me to stay home from school, came forth once again. Becoming riddled with unimaginable fright, seeing him sitting in the living room reading the newspaper; lights dim and the volume in the rest of the house set on mute, I shook uncontrollably. Normally there would be tantalizing aromas from mommie's cooking, and the banging sounds of dishes coming from the kitchen, or the blasting rhythms of music traveling down the stairwell out of Chandler's bedroom, but never the numbing sounds of quiet. Standing with my back leaning against the front door, looking at him smiling like a evil villain, I turned to walk out the house, but before achieving this goal, his voice rang out, "where do you think

110   Brenda M. Files

you're going young lady?!" Nervous, my mouth could release only one thing, "where's mommie?" while thinking, 'please God, not again.' Without saying a word, he got up, walked over to where I stood saying, "questions in this house comes only from me!" Feeling his breath traveling down the back of my neck, I could smell he had been indulging in his favorite alcohol beverage, vodka, I became paralyzed. Moving closer into my personal space, pressing his private body part against my back saying, "since we know who is the ruler in this house, know that my voice will be heard! Now, answer my question! where do you think you're going?" Unsure of what to say, I began to beg, "daddy please don't," my tears flowing like a waterfall.

"Daddy please don't; what?! Don't ask me a question?! Don't be mad at me, or daddy please know that I'm sorry for not answering your question?! Just what am I suppose to please you with?!" Afraid to answer him, but more afraid not to since he wouldn't respect anything said, I strongly stated, "Please be a dad, not the monster who resides in your mind." He grabbed a handful of hair, pulling my head backwards, demanding my view of the ceiling, I could feel my whole world crumbling from beneath me. Forcefully, turning my head to have a slight view of him standing behind me, I stared into the depth of evil; smelling the stench of alcohol blasting across my nose; my mind rolling back the curtains of my short life to a time of laughter, sitting at the dinner table with my family, and the man carving the meat, who was once my father. Having nothing left to save me from his wrath, I started praying for God to send mommie home. Unfortunately this did not happen, instead I traveled down a long path, deep into a hellish nightmare. "I guess you have a problem answering me, or you're so grown you won't answer the question? Since you won't answer, I have a remedy for this." This statement made me even more nervous, but I didn't have to wait long to find out what he meant. Turning me around to completely face him, he firmly stated, "now Miss. I'm so grown; no longer a princess, march you behind up stairs!"

I didn't have a choice at this point, but to follow instructions; with a handful of my hair still twirled around the palm of his hand I began walking up the carpet lined stairs, listening to a few of them release songs of squeaks; humming I didn't want to ever cease. Once we reached the top landing and the singing staircase stopped its tune, my heart was racing so fast I became dizzy; my vision blurred. Before another second could pass, I felt a hearty shove; helping me to gain an unwelcomed visit with the floor. I quickly thanked God for carpet. Manhandling me as if I were a strange rag doll, bought from the second hand store, he demanded, "Get up; go into your room!" Prying my face from its visitation with the saving grace of floor covering, I got up without looking back and proceeded to do as commanded without saying a word. Soon I was standing at the door of what would be a room of mayhem. Frozen like a statue, suddenly I heard the roar of another command. "What are you waiting for; open the door!" Creating a small window of hesitation in lack of cooperation, the hand of this wicked monster standing in the background, reached around me, opened the door for its self, and gestured for me to enter inside. With only a second contributed to strong willed; being pragmatic, I tried once again to convince this madman, to see me, his daughter.

Turning around, I looked into his eyes pleading, crying out for mercy. "I'm so sorry daddy!" A name I hated to use in connection with him, "I'm so sorry for acting grown; making you angry! I truly didn't mean to hurt you! Please

Brenda M. Files

forgive me! I promise never to be disobedient, or disrespectful again! Will you please, please forgive me this time for breaking your rules?!" Starring at me for a short period before responding, he finally stated in a unrecognizable voice, "I know you're sorry, now take your clothes off!"

"What?!" I asked in surprise.

"Have you lost your hearing also?! I said.....take your clothes off, and don't make me ask again, or I will take them off for you!"

"But I don't understand."

Pushing me into hell; him following close behind, turned me around to be face to face, immediately the buttons of my blouse were ripped with great force away from its fabric, scattering them across the room. Releasing a loud yell, I quickly grabbed, and struggled to regain control of my clothing. With much effort, I tried to pull the shirt back together, hoping to shield his view of my exposed body parts. Troubled by this reaction, the stranger wrestled my hands away; taking away any comfort of being covered; forcefully ripping the remaining fabric completely from my upper body. Pushing me onto my bed, he stood there looking for a few seconds with a slight smile drawn across his face, rubbing his chest and licking his lips, no longer resembling the man who raised me. Having no thought of me, or my painful outcries, clearly separated from my welfare, he started to franticly pull at my pants, inducing me to kick aimlessly toward his body; trying to fend off the unfamiliar beast residing in him. In the meantime, I yelled disrespectful words. "Get away from me you derange, #!#!# evil monster!" Becoming increasingly agitated, he snatched me from the mattress as if I was a sheet of paper, pulling the comforter along with me.

Covering my mouth with his hand, his eyes bulging, teeth clinched, he angrily said, "If you want to disappear today after we're finished, always remember I will have your sister to take your place." Quickly I stopped my resistance, and listened to whatever he had to say. "Now that I have your full attention, I am going to remove my hand from your mouth, but if there is even a hiccup, your neck will snap like a twig, and your mother and sister will find your dead body lying at the bottom of the stairs. Do you understand me?" I nodded, 'yes.'

Placing me back on the bed, he demanded me to take off my pants, but evidently I was moving too slow, when he aggressively removed the garment without permission. Shattered by grief, I laid there motionless, waiting for the next episode to take place. Lying down next to me, he began rubbing my legs and breasts, causing me to feel as if I was looking at some bad movie not rated for television, or under age viewing; unfortunately for me, I had been picked to be the co-star of this porn flick of horror. With much effort, I tried to fight back the tears as he took away my innocence, my childhood.

Trying to get through this nightmare, I repeated inwardly several times, 'this is not happening, while thinking, I'd rather it be me and not my sister Chandler.'

As if fondling was not enough, he made the decision to get undressed, mount me and place his manhood inside my secret garden. Screaming in severe, excruciating pain; wiggling to free my trapped body, my tears increased in such a heavy flow I could feel the bedding beneath me dampening with moisture. Eventually, by the grace of God, the sociopath who was trying to rape me stopped; he could not complete his devious deed, due to great difficulty. Without haste, I silently gave thanks and all praises to my

Brenda M. Files

God above for saving me. Although in his warped, confused mind, the sounds of my screams and emotional tears made him believe everything displayed, was a signal of being very pleased. Horrified by this perplexed situation, time trapped me inside a hour glass of drowning sand, suffocating me slowly with its flow, no matter the end it stood on.

When all he could do was done, he got up from the hot bed of hell, stood at its foot, commanding my eyes, and ears to be opened to look, and listen to whatever he had to say. Although I found this task difficult, because he was standing there completely disrobed, I followed his order. "You were a good girl today once we removed the stubborn streak you had developed. You are definitely my sweet, and favorite child. But I need to remind you, if anyone find out about our father, daughter love secret, bad things will happen to your mother, and sister. Besides, they wouldn't understand, they will become jealous, and try to split us apart; we don't want that do we?" Having learned from my past mistake, I simply nodded, no.

"Since we agree, and you know how much I love you, get up so we can take a shower together." Startled by the term together, I hesitated to get up, fearing the harm that would come next. Once standing, I turned to look at the place where the evil deed happened, noticing not only the water marking of tear stains redesigning the bed sheets, but trails of bloody patches, causing a uncontrollable, loud gasp to escape from my lips. Giving misguided comfort, he tried reassuring me with disturbing words, "don't you concern yourself with what you see, it's only a symbol of our love. Our love is just like the day Jesus was pierced in the side as he hung on the cross bleeding water, and blood for our sake. He made the sacrifice, because of the love He has for us; our sacrifice today has the same representation as His divine love."

Quickly I grew angry; appalled that this insane person would compare his madness with my Savior, and the love He has for His children; but couldn't say anything in rebuttal. Still speaking he went on to say, "Our love has only allowed me touch the beginning of our connecting point; we'll soon connect all the way." Fortunately, I could no longer hear him: only thinking of two things, being forever destroyed inside, and my mother discovering I had become pregnant for a man I once called, daddy.

Once we showered, he gave instructions on how to get the blood out of the devil's linen; reluctantly I complied. When all of these missions were completed, fearfully wondering what was next, to my surprise he said, "by the way, I forgot to tell you, your mother, and sister left home for dinner and a movie right before you arrived. They wanted you to go with them, but since you were not here, I told them to go ahead, enjoy their evening, promising to make sure you have something to eat; let's go to the kitchen." Responding, I stated in a soft tone, "Thank you, but I'm not hungry."

"I am! I'm going downstairs to make me a sandwich." Upon leaving the room, he suddenly turned around to face me, saying in the same wicked tone of voice he used earlier, "make sure you take those sheet out of the washer, and put them in the dryer! You will also, make sure the bed is remade with the same linen before your mother, and sister return from their girl's night out, if you know what's good for you!" Remaining silent, he yelled, "Do you understand me?!" Once again, I simply nodded, 'yes.' When he departed, I locked the door behind him, fell to the floor, and wept.

Brenda M. Files

About a half hour later, I heard the front door slam; running over to the window of my bedroom, I pulled back the blue curtains to view my rapist walking down the sidewalk, leaving our home. Although, not being quite sure of what he would do next, I hastily closed the window dressing so he couldn't see me watching him. Hiding like an escapee from prison, I pressed my back against the wall and stood there for a few minutes to make sure the coast was clear. Finally hearing his car door slam, I immediately peeped out the window to make sure he was leaving; relieved, I thanked God to see his car drive away. No longer fearing he was anywhere near the house, I fell on my knees, praying in a soft voice, because wickedness could still be lurking somewhere nearby.

"My dear God, creator of heaven and earth, a God whom I worship, and adore, a God who will give peace in the middle of a storm, a God I serve, in Him I serve alone, You said in Your word that I have not, because I ask not, well Lord, I am asking. Lord, I am Your child living under the roof of what use to be a place of safety, but now it has become a treacherous war zone. Tell me, what do I not do, what do I not say? Tell me Lord, where do I go to feel safe again, and whom do I trust? Lord, please send me a angel to protect me from a man I once knew. And Lord please protect my si......"

Immediately, I knew God heard my cry, when without warning, a very familiar voice rang out loudly in the background: it was my mother calling my name. Staying silent, I forced her to come up the stairs to find me, and my trembling body. Finally a knock came on my door, but I still said nothing. However, a few moments later the door opened to pleasingly allow my mother, and sister walk inside. With happiness, my sister ran into the room, leaped on the bed like a trapeze artist, bouncing all around the mattress where I had position myself, while innocently asking, "where have you been? I wanted you to go with us," as I began to cry. Feeling she may had ignited a fire; believing I was afraid our mother was angry with me, Chandler ceasing her gymnastics maneuvers, to do her best in giving me consolation. Sitting down next to me on what use to be a cushion of restful comfort, she held me tight in her arms saying, "I'm so sorry to upset you, but I want you to know, no one is mad with you, not even mommie, not even me. We're just glad to know you are home safe."

Suffering from time loss, I couldn't remember what time they left me alone for the night, allowing me to fall into a peaceful nights rest. Awaken by the bright sunlight streaming through my bedroom window, announcing it was morning, a new day's birth; regaining my faculties, I shivered in fear when I realized I hadn't done as instructed, but thankfully no one asked why my bed was absent of linen. Shortly thereafter, a knock came upon my door, causing me to shake; soon learning it was my mother when she said my name through the slight ajar in the door. When she entered my room; afraid her husband was somewhere near, I gathered the blanket someone had thrown across my body for warmth during the night, and placed it closely around my neck. Racing over to sit on the bed next to me, I could see she was visibly shaken by my reaction. Embracing and cradling me like a baby against her breast, she gently whispered in my ear. "Sweetie, tell mommie what's wrong?" Frighten, I hurriedly ask, "Where is dad?"

"He's not here, he has already left for work. But if you need him I will call, and get him home as quickly as possible."

Brenda M. Files

"No, don't call him!" I screamed; grabbing her arms to keep her from leaving my side: setting off inside her, a overwhelming alarm. "Don't worry Taylor, like Chandler told you last night, no one is angry with you, not even your dad."

While looking deep into her eyes, tears running down my face, trying in great effort to speak, I found it fruitless to do so at that particular moment. After many sniffles had been announced, water released, and nasal passage cleared, I gained the ability to speak; mommie was more than ready to listen. Shaking, I told her everything that transpired between me and the stranger; from beginning to end. Going against her heart, in the same hour, she placed me and my sister in a safe, secured home, in another town, leaving her sad and heavily burden, because once again she gave her children away for their protection. Dismissed from all of his children, the monster didn't try to learn where we were located, or if it was possible to find us; in reality he didn't care. Unfortunately for us, our mother died and sadly we never saw her alive again, nor allowed to attend the funeral. However, there is a bright side to this dysfunctional situation......my rapist left me, and my sister alone, all because of the courageous strength of our mother."

"Junior, hearing these words spoken about the character of a beautiful women, and how this mad man is still living, leading a life without regrets, I began to weep for Taylor, and Chandler."

CHAPTER TEN

" Son.......whenever I have thoughts about Peggy's qualities as a lady, and the mistreatment she had to endure, causes my body to become permeated, completely infiltrated by anger, fueled by a will to destroy Thomas in slow torture. In the meantime, while trying desperately to lift the blinding veil of corruption from my mind, I gave my undivided attention to Taylor as she continued to share her devastating, life changing experiences."

"Mr. Charles, my rapist did a lot of cruel things not only to me, but he leaves behind a trail of victims, male and female, but by the grace of God he did not reach my sister, until now, fortunately it was not sexual. Mr. Charles, my mother was embarrassed to have married such a monster; living in the same house, sleeping in the same bed with this person for years, and knowing nothing of his secret life. Because of her worth, I want to see justice prevailed for her death, I want someone to be apprehended, placed in prison for life, or given the same fate as my mother.....death.

My mother deserves to have her name cleared from rumor stains of being killed by a lover, or suicide. She would never cheat, or take her own life. This would be against her moral values, unlike the man who was once the head of our household and is now the head of your ex-wife. Before my mother met you at the mall, she found a way to leave information for me with her attorney. This is how I learned your wife helped this maniac in every aspect of his wicked behavior, making my mother's daily walk in life a living nightmare. Even though she wasn't there in the beginning of his deranged behavior, and surely didn't create the monster inside of him, she did however, nurse, aid, and perpetuated his path of destruction. This less than human,

Brenda M. Files

started his serial, criminal acts at the young age of thirteen as far as we know. One day with a knife in his hand, he threaten bodily harm toward his younger sister Jane, forcing her to become fully undressed, lie down on their parents bed with her open legs for his viewing pleasure. In the beginning there was only looking, and touching, whenever opportunity presented itself, never failing to remind his victims about sharing secret to anyone unless they disliked living; each victim readily obeyed every word of his demands.

However, on one particular day safety came in the form of their younger brother Grant; saving his sister from ongoing torture that was done by Thomas. In her sight Grant was a guardian angel with hidden wings; expanded wide, and long when it was time for her to be protected. Thomas had been left alone with her for what was presumed to be several hours; immediately after the family departed, he began his sexual assault. This time his plans were to go further in his escapade of incestuous abuse. Instead, his sister battled with him in effort to protect herself from his madness; knocking over a lamp when he threw her against the nightstand, causing it to crash to the floor; gave no deterrence, but quickly gained the attention of their young brother Grant as he approached the front entrance of the home. In the next moment Thomas without awareness, was abruptly removed from atop of Jane, and flung to the floor. Immediately following this action, she heard the voice of her younger brother saying, "have you lost your mind, you crazy son-of- a- dog," while pounding him steadily with fists of fury. Now, it was Thomas time to cry out for help.

After all was over, about a week later, the siblings formed a pact for change, promising never tell their parents about what had taken place on that ugly day; in order to protect the family from shameful hurt. They knew this ugliness would disgrace the family' name forever. After that day Thomas never touched Aunt Jane again, especially when he knew Grant could be lurking somewhere nearby. Even though Grant was younger than Thomas, his fist were mightier. Nevertheless, in the end Aunt Jane was never the same again, committing suicide a few months later....or so they say. Grant never believed Jane had taken her life, and prayed Thomas had nothing to do with her demise; believing otherwise. With him having no proof, he never shared these thoughts with anyone until the day he found it more than necessary.

As the years passed, Thomas convinced his brother to somehow believe, he had gotten the professional help needed for his uncontrollable, predatory addiction; was now cured. Eventually, Thomas went off to college, later joining the military, where it was later discovered his ways had never changed; his reign of terror had only just begun.

Then, along comes your wife, like a vicious, infection ready to help him promote increasingly, deranged behavior; in subhuman devastation.

From the beginning of their relationship, most people in our family believed Kandi injected herself as a toxic poison, inciting his deviant behavior for her own pleasure, but I knew he guided her into his corruption of evil, including murder. This man has been sick for a very long time; doing anything to satisfy his self indulging pleasures, even placing our brothers up for adoption. I just didn't know how deep his wickedness could go, or the negative effects he had on our family life. We are one ugly, life of lies. I want to find my brothers, and reunite with them, but my rapist has made it difficult, because each were closed

Brenda M. Files

adoptions. Mr. Charles, for the sake of me, and my sister we need to know who they are! Because, what if we meet, fall in love, and possibly marry our own brothers?

Unfortunately and fortunately for me, the most hurtful, but wonderful thing happened in my life during this out of control, fictional, true life story. I've already found myself deeply in love with my own brother! Let's talk poetic justice shall we! And no, it isn't one of the adopted, missing brothers, but I am....in love with your son! Your youngest son Terrence is the man I'm in love with, and he is my brother! Oh I'm sorry, I mean my rapist son!"

Pausing for a few second to breath, she gathered her thoughts. "How could this be kept a secret?! How could no one see the catastrophe that was bound to happen?! especially with all of us dwelling in close proximity of one another! How could no one see that there was a great possibility we may meet, and maybe fall for in love?! Why didn't someone negotiate, or navigate our future for safety reasons, after this adult disaster?! Tell me, how does evil continue to exist at such a high level among us?! Please, tell me why did Terrence, and I receive the worst hand; dealt from the bottom of the deck?!"

Completely stunned concerning Terrence, and Taylor's involvement with one another, I didn't know what to say. At this point, all I wanted to do was reenact the life of Francis Augustus Hamer, a Texas Ranger who introduced the final act in the lives of Bonnie Parker, and Clyde Barrow. However, this scene would feature Thomas, and Kandi in the leading roles for the dramatic climax in the grand finale of massive bullet firing. I knew something needed to be injected into the conversation to help relieve the mounting pressure from Taylor's rising, hematoma of anger: lovingly I touched her on the arm and gave a slight smile saying, "I'm so sorry to interrupt your sharing time; possibly making you lose your thoughts, but I couldn't wait any longer to speak because your questions are very valid for the adults involved in this horrific mess, including me. Although I have no answers as to why this happened, or why we didn't come forth with the truth in order to help in prevention, but we have to deal with the mess we've created for our children. Unintentionally, my hands are included in a dirty situation I'm embarrassed to claim any part of its ownership. For everything, I am so sorry."

After sharing the things her mother allowed me to know about Terrence, and Diamond not being my biological children, I reassured Taylor, "no matter what, they are still my children; nothing, not even the flow of DNA running through our blood, could change this fact." Without apology she declared, "I'm so sorry this happened to you Mr. Charles, but I must ask, why didn't you tell them when you found out about this ugly deception? Didn't you think they deserved to know?"

"Of course they deserved to know. By the time I learned of the underhanded things concerning Kandi, and Thomas affair, all my children except Junior., had been brainwashed against me, readily accepting, and believing whatever their mother told them about the break-up of our family. Although devastated, I didn't think it was necessary to disgrace, or humiliate their mother, bringing more confusion into their lives. Even with proof of infidelity between Kandi and Thomas, instead of using this to derail what has been told about the failure of our marriage, I allowed each to become independent thinkers."

"Well please tell me, what's left for the children to do, who found the pathway to the dungeon of doom? What do we do with the love we innocently found? Do we disregard the feelings we share? Do we say, oops we're sorry for our mistake, because of your mistake? At least tell me if we should continue with our forbidden love, get married, eventually produce inbreeds of undesirable children that will be criticized, and ostracize by the world, because of secrets? You may not have the answers, but there is one thing for sure, Terrence and I will never think about giving each other up, no matter the blood line. Now, if there is anyone who wants to be against us, can go straight to the place they created for us...hell!!"

After looking into my eyes for a short period, I knew her anger was not being unleashed on me intentionally, but I was available; one of the adult headlined in this chronicle of disaster, to hear what was on her mind. "By the way, I allowed Terrence to read most of the lengthy letters from my mother's confessionals concerning all of the treasonous acts placed in our family. Like me, he did not take any of it very well; matter of fact he was downright fuming when he stormed out of the house earlier today. Since then, I have not been able to contact him; leaving countless messages left for him to call me back. That brings me to the reason I am here Mr. Charles, I'm really afraid of what he is thinking, or what he may, or may not do at this point. I need help finding your son."

I was more than willing to stand by the side of a young girl who had grown into a woman, but a real champion for any of her efforts, stating, "I will do whatever is needed to help find your boyfriend and my son."

Getting up from the brown leather sofa, I stood in front of the distraught young lady, extended my hand to receive hers, praying the gesture would be welcomed. Looking up with sadness etched across her face, a few seconds passed; filling me with dismal despair as I readied myself to retract my hand from the pit of humiliating rejection. A few more seconds ticked away from the clock when finally, her look soon delivered and granted a very pleasing smile as she slid my hand tightly inside of hers, accepting it in pure friendship. Pulling herself up from her seated position, slightly assisted by me, she stood tall as we headed out to locate our beloved Terrence.

Following a long night, and early morning hours of exhausting, fruitless scouring of the earth, we finally pulled up in front of the home belonging to the family who graciously allowed Peggy to secure her daughters with them, people who told the now deceased mother, "never to have any worries about their safety," promising to treat them as their own and provide a place of peace.

After exiting my car, I walked toward the passenger side of the vehicle, opening the door for my sleeping co-pilot to go inside and get some proper rest. Whispering her name softly, gently awakening her from unknown dreams, she sweetly ask,

"Mr. Charles, did I fall asleep?" Smiling, I politely answered, "yes sweetheart, but we're somewhere you love waking up. Let's get you inside your home," she too, began to smile.

Extending my hand to help her out of the car, the assistance was graciously accepted. Once we were standing outside the car, she stood in front of me, pleasingly stating, "thank you for helping me with everything," then kissed me on the cheek. Appreciating the warm gesture, I said enthusiastically, "No thanks necessary. Remember, we have the same love one missing, and since the love one we are looking for needs to be found, we are the team to do it, don't you think?"

Brenda M. Files

With a wide grin on her face, her voice rang in excitement, "Yes I do!"

Walking toward the front porch of the home, suddenly we were startled by the sound of a familiar voice in the stillness of the darkness in the early morning hours, calling out her name in the shadows,

"Taylor! I've been waiting for you!"

It was my son! A son I had not seen in many years. Looking at him made me proud to be his father as he stood there tall, muscular built, and very handsome. Dressed in a white tee shirt, blue jeans and leather sneakers; he was magazine cover ready. His skin was naturally a shade of light, tan of golden; his hair, thick curls of sandy brown locks, and his teeth white enough to light up the darkness in the early morning hours.........Terrance was now a man, he is my son.

Overjoyed, she shouted in happiness, ran up, latched onto his neck, gave him a long heartfelt kiss; forgetting my presence. I stood in the background waiting.

Soon she released him asking, "Terrence where have you been? We have been looking for you most of the night, and part of the morning!"

Replying with anger, "We? Do you mean the stranger standing next to you? The man who has pretended my entire life, to be my father?"

Allowing no room for my rebuttal, Taylor took over the wheel. Removing her arms from around his neck, she took a couple of steps backwards for a full view of his face, and every part of him saying, "Wait a minute Terrence, you just hold on! You know how much I love you, and would stand with you against anything, anybody, anywhere, but we have had this thing all wrong. First of all, the man that you are calling a stranger is one of the best thing we have as true family. Secondly, he has taken all of his time to help me look for you, carrying just as much loving concern for your safety as I have. Last but not least, he was also in the dark about not being your biological father, but disregarded facts claiming you were not his own. He won't allow a DNA test to dictate who's from his flesh, or his blood! This is a man we should readily accept inside our small world of confusion. This man is your father, no matter what your mother, or my rapist did against us!

I think an apology is owed, and should be given to Mr. Charles for disrespecting him for all those lost years you, and your siblings left him out in the cold to side with untruth!" After the long tongue lashing, Taylor placed her hands on her hips, waiting patiently for a response. In the meantime I remained quiet, standing in awe of her for not holding back, stating everything with a tremendous amount of confidence.

Silence blanketed the porch as we stood there; not even the sound of a cricket, or a bird chirping in the background could be heard as the sun began to perch on top of the mountains for its daily guard duty over the earth, while waiting to hear my son say something. Finally, after the shame evaporated, heaviness melted from his tongue, and his vocal cords had the ability to release sound, he walked over, stood tall in front of me, swallowed hard, took in a deep breath and collapsed in my arms, weeping uncontrollably.

Immediately we dissolved into a love fest, melting into each other like ice on a hot summer sidewalk.

Embracing my son tightly with arms of purity, Taylor completed the circle by joining in on the love connection.

Brenda M. Files

Restraining his emotions, trying hard to manage the sniffles, Terrence found the ability to whisper into my ear, words I longed to hear.

"Dad....I am so sorry. Please forgive me. And please believe; I still and will always love you, I was just angry."

After releasing our embrace, he stepped back, "before either of you say anything, I need to say something very important. Earlier, I had murder on my mind, I had it against Thomas for what he did in our lives, I wanted to kill him!"

Leaving me without words to say behind his statement, rapidly Taylor asked, "Did you really have murder in mind? I ask, because I had the same feeling, but expelled the thought when I realized this wouldn't solve a thing, only bring more misery."

"Honestly.......I still want to kill him, after what he did to you. A person like that doesn't deserve to live. Sorry Taylor, sorry dad, but it's not easy for me to let it go!"

In the meantime, while lost in personal thoughts, I knew my sentiments were exactly as his. After an hour of discussions concerning our absence from one another, Taylor yawning and her eyes looking heavy, went inside to prepare for bed, agreeing to talk later. Meanwhile, I followed Terrence home where he was still residing with his mother. After parking his car in the driveway, he vigorously waved goodbye, before vanishing behind the large door as I slowly drove off with joy in my heart, a smile on my face, the two of them on my mind; headed for home."

Taking a deep breath, I paused from reading, because sadly, this was my father's last entry into the manuscript; the very next day someone tried to take his life. Two hours later, after taking a walk through the hospital long corridors and visiting the cafeteria for a bite to eat, before I curled up once again in the corner of the room where my father was still lying motionless under the white linens, and tubes traveling from his body, I kissed him gently on the forehead. Starting from the point where my father's words left off, I continued on this treacherous road of disaster by reading the documents and diary Peggy left behind.

However, before I could really get started, Taylor came barreling through the hospital door for a visit, sharing with me how hard Terrence was beating up on himself, due to shameful humiliation for not coming earlier to the hospital to visit our ailing father, "All Terrence want, is the love his family, show appreciation to the man who raised him, and return the love he was given, but afraid it is too late to share this with his dad."

Quickly I replied, "too late is after death when the love can't be seen, heard or felt; our father is very much alive and Terrence is welcomed to be here by his side.

Before departing company for the evening, I agreed to call my brother not only to make all of us feel better, but having another sibling standing here with me, would make me happy, and make our dad proud.

Brenda M. Files

CHAPTER ELEVEN

After a week of communication with my brother, I welcomed the loving visits from him and Taylor; always bringing so much joy, making things better during the long days at the hospital. They helped me not to have lingering animosity toward my absent sister Diamond, the sister who has made her where abouts very mysterious. As time crept slowly, early one morning shock was drawn across my face when the door suddenly swung open, and Taylor came racing into the hospital room looking as if she had seen a ghost. Her skin resembled a person hidden away in darkness, never to have been kissed by the sun, or in serious need of a blood transfusion.

Running briskly up toward me, she collapsed into my arms crying inconsolably; sniffles interrupting each word she blared out. "The police came by your mother's home last night; they arrested Terrence! They put him in handcuffs, and drove away!"

By this time, the hospital door swung open once again, but this time it was the nurse on duty in charge of my father's medical care, quite annoyed by our presence.

Instantly, the embrace between us melted, her loud hiccup conversation simmered down as the nurse declared in a demanding, low, monotonic voice, "please bring your volume down, or leave the room, or the hospital altogether, but whatever you do; do it now! It doesn't matter what your decision may be, but when it comes to my patient, I will not allow anyone, no matter their relationship, disrupt the care given!"

Dancing around the bed tending her patient, she gently fluffed his pillows, adjusted his sheets, checked his vitals, and moisten his lips, bringing comfort to the needs of a man I call dad. The entire time she stayed focused, never looking at either of us, but needless to say, we had no doubt who were the targets for her strong words of corrections.

The presence of the nurse, and her voice of authority, successfully quelled the excitement of Taylor's hysteria. Quickly grabbing her by the hand, ushering us out of the private arena of medical treatment, we took the latter part of the nurse's advice, hopped on the first available elevator guiding us to down stairs; out of the hospital. Once outside, my eyes squinted as the sun shined brightly upon my face, and the feel of wind releasing, brisk, echoing breezes, that swayed trees from side to side, causing fallen leaves to dance in circular motions, yielded me much appreciation for the outdoors. It was a beautiful, crisp, refreshing, spring day to enjoy God's beauty; beauty I have been absent from, and missed for a very long time. Finally we found our way to the patio where most employees gathered together for lunch, or shared break time, and to our surprise the sitting area was almost void of people, yielding much privacy for the two of us to talk. With tears never retracting their steady flow, Taylor began telling me what happened once again, but this time, calmly; absent of any hysterical drama. "Your mother called me saying the police came to her home in the late evening not long after I left; taking Terrence to jail on the suspicions of something he wouldn't do."

"Suspicions of what?" I ask in a strong tone, fearing the unknown.

"For the murder of my rapist," whispering her words while leaning forward and looking around to make sure no one was close enough to hear her tell dirty families secrets.

Stunned by the announcement that Thomas was dead, not to mention accusing my brother of the crime, I was

Brenda M. Files

lucky there was a bench nearby; without thought, lowered my body onto its seat. Speechless, I clasped my hands together, looked down at the earth, saying nothing. After lengthy time had passed, finally able to formulate words to reciprocate, I looked up from my dismal frustration. Taylor standing there waiting with her arms folded against her chest, head tilted to one side, the wind blowing constantly, sweeping her hair into her face as she continued to gaze in my direction, patiently waiting for a response. Nervously, I finally replied, "Taylor I am so sorry to hear what happened to your dad..." interrupting me in mid-sentence, firmly stating with displeasure drawn on her face, "Well I'm not! And please, never put me in a position to say this again, that man is not my dad, so stop addressing him that way! He is a rapist! What we should be concerned about is Terrance, your brother, my love, being locked up behind bars!"

Dismissing the reprimand, "what happened to make them think Terrance did this to Thomas?"

"From what I understand, after finding his dead body the police have a couple of witnesses who've stated they saw Terrence leaving that man's home. I did have the opportunity to talk with Terrance after he had gone to see Thomas, but failed to tell me he would be going to see him again. He knew I wouldn't agree with this decision. Now scared stiff he's freely repeating, "your dad is dead, but I found him that way! I give you my word, I found him that way!"

I was shaking like a leaf, not because of fear, but permitting Terrence to call Thomas my dad. Instead, with loving honesty I replied, "I know you didn't hurt him, nor could you hurt anyone, but I need to know where he is, and why were you there?"

"He's at his home, lying on the floor in his living room with blood running from everywhere, especially around his head. I've never seen so much blood! I went to his home to ask him why did he do all those terrible things to you? But with hindsight being a great teacher, I know now it was a foolish mistake! I just wanted to look into his eyes, and hear what he had to say, even though it's known he couldn't tell the truth if his life depended on it. Taylor, I'm sorry, but for some reason, I just wanted to hear what he had to say."

In that instance she said, "we have to call the police! But we must always remember, no matter what the police think, believe, say, or do , we do not talk to them without the presence of an attorney."

"But when they question me, wanting to know how I knew a crime had been committed; was I there? then what? What will I tell them?"

"We will tell the truth."

"Then they will accuse me of hurting Thomas, because I was in his home with no earthly reason for being there, besides accusation against him. On the other hand, they'll have substantial amount of motives against me. For this alone I will go to jail. Let's not forget, I am a black man, and the deceased is white....what more will the law need to arrest me? By the way, I've saved the best for last, the dead man is a highly ranked General representing the military, who's secretly been my mother's lover and my father! How poetic is this justice!"

"It doesn't matter who they think he is, or what he pretended to represent, if they have no evidence there is no way they can charge you with anything. You just happened to be in the wrong place at the wrong time."

With his eyes pleading, Terrence said, "but I found the body, and I ran away from the scene of the crime."

Taylor with confidence interjected innocently, "with our unity, the world will know power!" Embracing her repeating, "I'm so sorry!" over and over again.

Listening to this distraught young lady, I stood up from the bench, placed my hands in my pockets, and walked a few paces away from where she stood.

A short time later, I turned to face her again saying, "do you know where Terrence mother is located?"

Before she answered, I dismissed the thought of calling the lady who is suppose to be our mother, because I knew this conversation was to important to be held over the phone. Coming out of my distracting fog, I heard Taylor say boldly, "when I left her home crying, right before coming here; emotionally devastate about losing her love one to death in such a catastrophic, senseless way. Her words not mine. To tell the truth, she didn't seem concerned for her son being carted off to jail."

"Well one thing for sure, Thomas has only himself to blame, and my brother isn't guilty of his overdue murder."

"That for sure, and I will not stop my search for the culprits who did this crime, and the right person is behind bars. Most of all, to shake the killer's hand for doing an honorable service for me, my sister and the general public; saving us from madness." Startled, but not surprised by her honesty, I removed my hands from my pockets, reached over, pulled her close, whispering in her ear,

"you can count on me to be with you every step of the way." After kissing her on the forehead, she looked up into my eyes smiling, laid her head against my chest, finding it a pillow of comfort. We stood there hugging, consoling each other for a very long time.

The next morning after having a lengthy conversation with Taylor about our next step to help exonerate Terrence,

I vacated my position next to the best man in the world, in hunt for the truth. With bad intent, one of my stops for the day was to give a impetuous visit to our invisible mother at her home.

Several hours after sharing a beautiful morning with my brother, lunch with Taylor, I looked down to find my feet planted on the door mat placed at the threshold of my mother's house that read, 'Warm Welcome To Visitors.' I laughed out loud at the humorous, irony of the floor sign; not reflecting the real truth of the occupant. After ringing the doorbell several times, she finally decided to answer yielding only a small crack in the door to allow a minimal portion of her pupil to be seen; gaining a slight view of her visitor. Once she realized it was me, hurriedly she removed the security of her safety chains, swung the large frame of wood open, leaped and latched onto my neck for dear life, crying out loudly, "my son, my son, my son!" Totally caught off guard by her reaction, I failed to reciprocate with an embrace, instead I pulled my face away from her cheek; shamefully causing her hold around my neck to be released. Walking briskly past her, I went into the masterfully decorated living room, took a seat in the nearest chair, crossed my legs and waited on her to follow behind me, purposely she decided to take a seat on the off white, custom made sofa, across the room from me. Politely, from where I had chosen to take a seat, I got up, walked over to the sofa, sat closely beside her; wanting desperately to hear every word this lady had to say. If needed, I would be close enough to have the ability to read her lips, and promote hand signals; a substitute for sign language. Annoyed, I angrily ask, "Please tell me why you......as Terrence mother, haven't been to the jail to see him? Tell me why

Brenda M. Files

didn't you call me to let me know about his arrest? At least, tell me what's been going on in your mind?"

"What's been going on is this fact, the love of my life, the man I was going to marry, was killed, murdered in cold blood! I know my family did not care, or liked him, particularly after the secret meetings held with your father, allowing him to feed invalid information into Terrance system concerning Thomas. This has caused me to remain in solitude, alone in my private pain. From what I hear, my son Terrance is totally on your side; recovering his fatherly, and brotherly love. I heard you have also gained a potential sister-in-law! Now you tell me, why should I call, see, or talk to any of you? I'm sure you all have come to conjoined conclusions that's not in my favor. I also feel, there is no need for you to know when, or where I decide to go, or not go. But since you are here I will say this,....I could barely get out of bed to receive you as company, how can anyone have expectations from me to make it all the way downtown to see anyone?" Spitting out venomous poison with each word spoken, complimented her selfish behavior as she starred without blinking. Aggressively I responded, while trying to be respectful, "shame on you as a mother. Everything you've said is about you, what you're feeling, or thinking, except for your concerns for a man who could care less about anyone besides himself. I can't believe you. How selfish can you be to use a lame excuse such as the inability to get out of bed for not going to see your son? Just knowing your son is locked behind bars should cause the adrenaline in your body to flow so rapidly; you'd forget about getting in the car; running leaps, and bound to visit him. By the end of the day you'll need a sedative to calm down so you can sleep. Normal people do this when they care about a love one."

Saluting Madness   137

"When did you become a psychologist; telling me what my body, or mind should do! That's what wrong Junior, you're always analyzing; judging things you don't know anything about, just like your low down father!

With anger brewing, I desperately tried to remain calm, and show no disrespect. "Lady, if you want me to have a decent conversation with you, don't bring my father up, and please don't address him in an incorrect description. If you do this for me we can continue to talk, otherwise it all ends now." Annoyed, she replied, "I am in mourning, because the most important thing to me is gone, so I don't give a ##!#!#! flip about your bedridden daddy. Take your inconsiderate, nice nasty behind away from here, and when you gather some respect, some feelings of love for me, come back then, and not before!"

"You know what, I feel sorry for you. I don't know what this person has on you for you to alienate your entire family except for Diamond, but if you do nothing else, find it in your heart to go see Terrance, he needs to know we are all standing behind him. I'm sure he's the one feeling alone. Oh I'm sorry, I should have asked.....you do believe in his innocence; don't you?" With the look of anger painted on her face she stood up, yelling every word, "how dare you ask me anything about what I think, or feel?! You've already proven you don't care! I guess it really is time for you go back to the hospital to baby sit your zombie father! Now get the hell out of my house, and leave me alone! Remember, when you regain your senses, bringing respect into my home, come back then with an apology in hand! "

Seething inside, I made the chose not to respond to her comment, but honor the request of leaving her home. Although I had hoped to see Diamond before departing, but due to the circumstances I gladly gave up the thought of a

Brenda M. Files

possible reunion. Walking me to the door, she opened it just as wide as when I arrived, but now the hostess was presenting me the way out. Without a hug in farewell, she continued to look down at the floor; clutching the door knob, waiting for me to walk past where she stood. With my feet planted on the doormat of what use to be a family home, I stopped, turned to look at her, saying with great assertion, "when you regain your senses, and want to visit Terrence, I would love to tag along." Never looking up from the hardwood floor to bid me a safe journey, she left me with a high volume blast from her deep rooted feelings of anger, by slamming the door in my face. In that moment I came to realize, my mother's words were correctly chosen when she told me to get the hell out of her house, because her house was one hellish place, and I was more than happy to leave her alone.

CHAPTER TWELVE

A week later, feeling drained from all of the heart wrenching things going on in our family; things so far out of control all I could do was cry. However, there was a bright side in this whole ordeal, I have a closer relationship with my brother; standing with me for our dad. In the meantime, Taylor was a lone soldier visiting him while I remained at the hospital caring for our father, learning all I could from the piles of wicked information I had inherited.

Fortunately for us while visiting my brother, behind persistence, and annoying demands for someone to recognize the injustice done for her mother, Taylor finally succeeded in gaining the attention of a couple of detectives by the names of, Madison Jemison, and Kendrick Holmes. Suddenly for some unknown reason, they began listening to her shared stories after looking closer at the documented information she had given them. Information leading them to a broader range of suspects, people with profound reasons of wanting Thomas dead.

Stopped by the two detectives in the dimly lit, grimy, cold, dingy corridor of the county jail where Terrence had been transferred, desiring to speak with her for a question and answer session, also permitted Taylor the opportunity to ask the protectors of the law a few questions of her own.

After announcing their reason for stopping her she ask, "tell me, what has caused you to revisit these things? Did you finally realize the insurmountable evidence given, showed how wrong you've been in your conclusions? Did it show there were a lot of people housing hate for Thomas, and wanted him dead!? Did you find that this info could possibly allow you to know, Terrence is indeed innocent?

Do you think the killer is still roaming free? If these things are too much to answer, tell me.....what took so long?!"

Reluctantly, Jemison gave a vague statement for their decision to follow these leads into their investigation. "We just needed fresh eyes and we don't want to leave no stones unturned. What we want is absolution."

"Absolution in what! finding the truth?! Absolution about the real culprit behind the murder of my mother, or absolution on allowing things to go in the wrong, darn direction......like the Charles Mallory's case?!"

Both detectives standing erect, said nothing behind the strong accusations against the police department for failing to do their job. Taylor simply replied, "hummm, just like I thought, nothing!"

Turning to leave, she threw one of her hands in the air, moving it from side to side in a waving motion; walking away shouting, "call me when you need help, but right now my hands are full, seeing about my love ones behind bars, and sick in the hospital! Have a good day!" leaving the detectives behind to give birth to any thoughts they desired.

Later that week, the detectives found their way to our mother's home to question her concerning their ongoing investigation, but found she was not there, but working.

Considering the embarrassment that may occur for the General if two civilian officers showed up on her job, they agreed to give her a call, allowing her ample opportunity to make an appointment for the interview, but if no time could be given, they would stick with the original plan of visiting the military base. She opted not for the latter. After a couple of hours, Kandi arrived home promptly at the appointed time to find the detectives parked and patiently waiting to have a few moments of her time.

Getting out of the vehicle before she could place the car in park, they preceded up the sidewalk leading to the front door of her home; waiting for her to join them. Gathering her purse from the passenger seat, Kandi exited the vehicle, pristinely dressed in her uniform; famously put on a public face consisting of a wide grin that resemble the animated cat Garfield. Making her way to give greetings; with her arm stretched forward and her hand wide open, the detectives accepted the polite, gesture of welcome. After the meet, and greet session was over, Holmes took the lead, "Ms. Mallory, thanks for allowing us this opportunity to speak with you."

"Sorry to correct your mistake, but my name is Douglas," she stated in a strong tone.

Noticing her facial expression changing drastically, Holmes asked, "now that the correction has been made, would you mind if we came inside to speak with you, Ms. Douglas? We hope not to take up to much of your time."

Clearing her throat she responded, "of course; follow me!"

Nervously she unlocked the front door; opening up her home for the two detectives inside, a few seconds later, she politely pointed; guiding them into the living room to have a seat. Showing hospitality she stated, "I'm going to have something to drink, is there anything I can get the two of you, a cup of coffee, a soda, or maybe a glass of water?" Immediately the two detectives answered in unison, "no thank you." Holmes added, "but, thank you for asking," while sitting in chairs positioned around the large room. In the meantime she left them to retrieve herself a drink. Reentering the room with a small glass of liquid in hand, she asked, "are you guys sure I can't get you anything to drink? There's nothing more refreshing at the end of a hard day's work, or during lunch, than a stiff drink of relaxing fluid; it helps to de-clutter the brain of excessive debris," while sitting down on the sofa.

"No ma'am, but one thing is for sure, alcohol is a way to drown unwanted, or wicked thoughts from the brain cells temporarily," Jemison sarcastically stated.

"Well it's a pleasure when someone agrees; who knows where you're coming from," Kandi replied.

"Yes ma'am," the detective stated, but within an instant said, "The reason we're here Ms. Mallory....I'm sorry, I mean Ms. Douglas."

"Since you're having difficulty remembering my name, just call me Kandi, with a K, ending in an i," yielding a fake sounding snicker behind her words. Finding no humor, Jemison continued, "Well Ms. Kandi, with a k and i....."

Agitated after having to clarify her name once again for them, she forcefully stated, "there is no need to add Ms. to my name, just Kandi will do!"

"Yes ma'am! Well Kandi, the reason for our visit, we need to ask you a few questions concerning a Ms...." stopping for a moment to flip open her notebook, rifling through a few pages to locate, and make sure the correct pronunciation rolled from her tongue before continuing. "Sorry for the delay, but her name is Ms. Janice Brooks."

Shaken by the name from the past, Kandi tried with difficulty to hid her trembling hand as she gripped the glass tightly, causing the contents to sway aggressively from side to side. The police had already ascertained the information concerning the rape, filed in a complaint by Janice Brooks, against Kandi Douglas, and Thomas Laskey.

Pretending to deeply concentrate, to regain total recall of the person in question, she looked toward the ceiling searching for a helpful response. Swiftly, she sat down on the sofa, before collapsing behind knocking knees, shaking legs, and the feeling of fainting from sheer nervousness.

Trying to recover her composure, but not completely successful in the attempt, she blurted out a thought believed to be a decent answer, "I'm not very familiar with the owner of that name, but I do recall hearing it floating around the base a time, or two. Why do you ask? Is she okay?"

"Well, from what we have learned, Ms. Janice Brooks brought a sexual harassment, and rape allegation against you and General Thomas Laskey, can you tell us if this is correct Kandi?" Deliberately, the detective surprised her with the loaded question to obtain a visible reactions for possible self incrimination: expecting her to be less than truthful.

Enjoying watching her squirm while Kandi sifted through her large container of lies, hoping for a flicker of light amid her multitude of darken secrets to help locate an answer; anything besides the truth. Jemison and Holmes calmly waited, knowing the longer the pause, there was something always hidden. They also knew, if this type of allegations has been made against someone's reputation, that person should be exploding in anger, defending their honor behind such a strong accusation. Soon realizing this error, she sought out a feasible answer for her late reaction. Hurriedly she stated a perilous lie, "this conversation, and your insulting questions are so beneath me, I hate trying to answer. I have no idea why anyone would accuse us of such a horrific, scandalous crime". After taking in a deep breath, a large gulp of the alcohol beverage, she continued, "when we learned of this treacherous act of falsehood, I demanded to confront the person bringing forth this hideous claim. However, this would not be, because the allegations were unfounded; no witnesses to support her malicious claim; the case died. Janice Brooks should be grateful we didn't bring a charge of defamation against her. So to remember her was the least of things I wanted to have occupying storage in my brain." Extending a quick, unpleasant smile, trying to display unhidden disdain for the detectives, she stood up saying, "now if you're finished with your reason for being here, there are people who depend on me; I need to get back to the base."

The confidence shown in Kandi's physical demeanor and her tone of voice, exude a rich thickness of arrogance, and disrespect against the two detectives. It was very obvious she believed Thomas had discarded the sexual recording they created together, never to be seen by anyone else, not even investigators of the highest caliber.

Having nothing solid to hold her on as far as the crimes they were looking into, Jemison glanced discretely at her partner, giving a slight nod of her head, and said in a sarcastic but polite tone, "Well Kandi, we do appreciate you being willing to leave all of the soldiers under your command, allowing us the opportunity to speak with you, but we still need......" Regardless of the kindness extended, Kandi wasn't pleased; promptly interrupting Jemison's statement. "How can you pretend to appreciate me; having the galls to ask questions irrelevant to the case concerning the murder of my fiancé?! How dare you come into my home with no concerns about what I'm feeling, or my loss?! Who could have thought that law enforcement would be so full of trickery; having the nerves to ask anyone, especially me, questions about a person who brought harm to mine, and Thomas reputation with lies?! You two came here just to add undue stress to a already god forsaken situation, instead of having your focus on Thomas's murderer. Shame on you!"

Without another word said between them, she walked over to the front door, opened it; ushering them out of her home. With her head turned away, she never looked at them again; waiting for their departure. Following the vivid instructions given, the two detectives stood up from their chairs, walked to the front of the house where Kandi stood and exited the home. Forcefully she slammed the large slab of oak in their face; not permitting another word to be spoken. Immediately the partners marched down the small flight of steps onto the sidewalk, piled into their car, heading for downtown headquarters,; agreeing Kandi was definitely a person of interest.

CHAPTER THIRTEEN

Earlier that week, the detective had shown up at the home of Janice Brooks, stationed at a local Army base in Georgia, to listen to her version about the rape allegation brought against the two General's. The day had been rainy and very gloomy as grey clouds cast darkness over the city, causing the noon day to resemble night, but didn't deter Janice from waiting and greeting them at the door of her small, wood frame home; landscaped with many colorful flower and large trees. Now divorced with no children, she was skeptical, and reluctant to a sit down in conversation with them, because of the treatment she endured in past times after trusting authorities of law. She relented.

Janice had adopted the belief that everything about the investigation had been designed to help protect Kandi and Thomas. She believed the police wanted to entrap her in lies behind any misused word, in effort to help exonerate the two people she knew raped, and sodomized her.

Although it didn't matter how skeptical people were about her truth, she was equipped with confidence, willing to stand against all negatives, regardless of denials made by the Brigadier General, or her claim of what happened inside her home. On that evening there were three things she knew for sure, she had been raped, something had been placed in her drink, and there was male semen inside her body, a perfect match to General Laskey. Strongly, Janice presented everything she had as evidence to the detectives.

Even though she was participating with the detectives, she had no idea recording had been made, and discovered, proving the alleged crime committed against her was true. This time Janice vehicle didn't run out of gas, this time efficiency cut the line that fueled her rapists crimes. When the detectives finally told Janice the General was dead, she sat motionless, crying tears of joy, but on the other hand she was sad he didn't go to jail so he could be raped over and over again. The detectives left her with the belief, there would be vindication.

Both detectives started believing without a doubt, the military had committed a large cover-up to protect people who didn't deserve to wear the uniform, or stand under the flag representing the United States of America.

The following day, after having a very informative, visit with Kandi and Janice, the detectives made an appointment, and was now arriving at the home of the Laskeys. However, this home was that of Grant Laskey, and his wife, Nancy. Regrettably, Grant was not readily in acceptance of them talking with their daughter Amy, who was now a beautiful young lady, very studious in her scholastic pursuits. Sadly, every day was still a constant battle for her to adjust to normal life, or gain personal friendships, always trying not to retreat into silence, due to her awkward communication skills. In the end, the final word for the interview was given by her mother Nancy, and Amy overriding Grant's objections.

Arriving on time, Holmes parked their car in front of the Laskey's home, but before going inside, Holmes stood outside of the car, peeled off his jacket, threw it across his forearm, wiping sweat from his face on such an unusual warm day as the sun hung high in the sky casting down angry, scorching heat upon the earth. Becoming anxious, he was hoping to take refuge inside the air conditioned home.

Before the detectives could ascend onto the porch, the door swung open, surprising the duo when they received overwhelming greetings from their gracious hostess, Nancy. The detectives appreciated the kindness, as she ushered them inside the cool comfort of their home with a pleasant smile.

"Please, come in; have a seat anywhere. May I offer either of you something to drink, or eat? I was about to prepare myself a cup of hot tea."

In acceptance of the invitation, Jemison exclaimed, "Yes, For me! I would love a good cup of tea!"

Unable to understand hot tea on such a warm day, Holmes humbly suggested, "thank you for your kindness, but if you don't mind, would you please make mine a tall, ice cold, glass of water."

"Of course detectives. I'll be right back with those orders," dismissing herself from the room, the two sat down and waited for the hostess return.

Shortly thereafter, walking slowly, Nancy entered the living area carrying a wicker tray with a large mug on it resembling a old fashion canning jar, engraved with the word 'ball,' across its glass face. The container was filled to its rim with ice, water, and two slices of lemons placed perfectly on its lip. She was also balancing two tea cups, a ceramic small pot, and containers housing cream, and sugar to serve her invited guest. Placing the well equipped transportation device on the table, she distributed each order into the hands of the person who made the request. Politely Nancy asked Jemison, "what would you prefer with your tea.... cream, sugar, or both?"

"Neither: I'm sorry to be a bother; do you have any sweeteners available?" she questioned. "No bother, because I have some right here." Unfolding one of the napkins on the tray, Nancy unveiled a few packets of sweeteners, and handed them to the detective. After taking a few sips from beverages, Holmes wanted to get back to the matter at hand. Interrupting their sweet sensations of tea connection, he said, "thank you so much for all of your kindness Mrs. Laskey, but if you don't mind, will you please allow us to speak with your daughter?"

"Yes you may, once her father arrives. I promised him that no one would question her unless he was present. I called him just before coming back in here and he is on the way. It will only take him a couple of minutes to get here, so enjoy your beverages while I let Amy know the two of you are here, and her father will be home soon."

By the time she made her way up the flight of stairs to speak with her daughter, Grant came pouring through the door, blaring words toward his wife, "Nancy I'm home!"

Slamming the door behind him, he made his way to where they were waiting, yelling "Where are you?"

Turning the corner, seemingly surprised by their presence, quickly regrouped and politely shook each hand extended. After all the introduction had come to a close, there appeared at the threshold of the doorway was Nancy, and their daughter Amy.

Amy was a tall, small framed young lady; well proportioned for her size, and height. Her wavy hair; cut and shaped into a beautiful, shoulder length bob, accented with large heavy bangs, cascading down; caressing the top of her eyelashes. She looked like a fashion model coming in for a photo shoot. Dressed casually in an oversized long sleeve, white shirt, light colored jeans; she strolled into the room in bare feet, seemingly lathered in self confidence. Greeting each detective with a handshake, Amy graciously displayed a broad smile, leaving no one in that moment, (if they didn't know) to believe she had endured so much ugliness most of her life.

After sitting down closely between her parents on the floral sofa, Holmes, and Jemison came to the conclusion;

Amy was only comfortable in the room with strangers when there are loving, arms nearby to protect her if it deemed necessary. Carefully approaching the subject; lifting the fabric of antique delicacy from the sealed vault of ugly memories of her past, the young lady looked down at her feet for a short period of time before speaking.

Finally ready, the detectives disallowed many pending questions during the course of their interview, granting Amy the lead in things she was ready to share. Their strategy worked. Taking hold of the reins, Amy became the controller of her ugly life story, no longer fearing the awful memories; she hoped to gain some inner peace.

"First of all, you should know I didn't have a choice about what happened to me."

In that instance, no one responded to the statement; everyone knew she was a innocent victim. Soon she was on a journey of painstaking memories, drenched with piercing, disturbing details. Tears began to saturate her eyes and face, while the sound of her voice cracked. However, never once, not even for a second did these temporary interference of understandable emotions stop, or slow her truth telling down.

Approaching the end of the horrific story, Amy said something that gave them a lead they were happy to follow up on. "On many nights; being held against my will in hotel rooms, and a few other places, I remember something very distinct about his co-conspirator, his partner in crime. Even though I never saw, or really heard the person speak except in brief goodbyes: her words left an impression, forever residing inside my head. I also have total recall of her fragrance; it always smelled so uniquely fresh.

On one particular day, while shopping in a upscale department store, waiting on the cashier to ring up my purchase up, I captured the same scent in my nostril as a unknown woman passed me by. I knew without a doubt, it was the same aroma. Frighten she could be the person who assaulted me, I decided to cast all fears aside, become bold enough to ask the name of the fragrance she was wearing; yielding not a moment in hesitation she told me, "loving essence."

In the next moment she walked away without looking back, or seemed to recognize me; leaving me to wonder if she was my rapist? This was something I needed to find out for my peace of mind; for stability sake."

Pausing, Amy stared at the floor for a few moments, seemingly to gather her thoughts, and as suddenly as she ceased speaking, she started the conversation again.

"I thought about that lady so much in that moment, I followed her throughout the store without being detected; at least not by her. However, a few customers and employees placed me under constant surveillance, believing I was trying to steal merchandise, by then I had become obsessed. I continued to keep this stranger on my scent radar, no longer giving thought to what others suspected of my actions.

Finally she left the store headed for her car, completely unaware of my presence. When she climbed in and before pulling out of the parking space, I had begun writing in my hand, the numbers from her license plate. Yes detectives, I was a stalker, so slap the hand cuffs on my wrist, place me under arrest for this crime!"

Detective Jemison regrettably interrupted, the sharing of her testimony for a few moments, "you are so refreshing young lady! In our field of work we hardly get anyone to tell the truth about wrong doing, or take ownership of it; not to mention, requesting arrest."

Brenda M. Files

"Thanks, but before you give compliments, I must admit to another crime. I became so determined to find out something about this lady, regardless of the consequences, I ask a friend of law enforcement to do me a favor. I asked this friend to acquire personal information from the tag number I had obtained. This person, who will remain nameless, because of their willingness to be helpful in my efforts, after learning the entire story of what happened to me. Even at the risk of losing their job. For this I am grateful, and will do all that is in my power to protect, and keep their identity safe. Like I previously stated, my wrists are free for handcuffs to be slapped on them at any given time."

Everyone started to laugh, including her parents. A few moments later, she continued telling her nightmare story.

"Anyway, during our investigation we learned this lady had been living in Hawaii with her family; pregnant several times throughout the years of my ordeals. Her husband's job transferred him and his family here, a few months ago. And I'm pretty sure I would have memories of a swollen belly brushing against my body.

This information brought me some relief, but added disturbance to my mind; realizing I had to go back inside a cave of unknown, and every woman once again, a suspect. Until one day when my father stopped for a few minutes to have a quick chat with a lady he knew, also handling business at the bank. Immediately, my nose latched onto the aroma of 'loving essence,' flowing from her well groomed, statuesque body, capturing my total attention. During the time they spent in conversation, I could tell she couldn't look me in the face, and was very uncomfortable in my presence. This extended me great pleasure knowing she was being tormented by many thoughts, wondering what, if anything, I may possibly remember.

However, it wasn't until I heard the familiar words she spoke after each encounter, did I know this was the lady I have been searching for: always leaving behind four words forever etched vividly in my mind, 'see you later hun.' I knew Kandi, without doubt, was the person helping my father's brother rape me on many occasions, once she said those same four words to me, and my dad as she departed or company! And I must say, I hate both of them. I'm glad Thomas is dead, and may Kandi have the same fate."

Silence consumed the room once Amy's words came to a close, and many trails of tears had been left behind. Both detectives not wanting to cause any further, emotional imbalance for the family, stood up to leave and granting Detective Jemison the opportunity to say, "I think we have heard enough to help us with our investigation. Thank you so much Amy for your cooperation, and thank you, Mr. and Mrs. Laskey for allowing us the time we needed to speak with your daughter. Now if you will excuse us, we will get out the way so you can enjoy the rest of the day."

Being a gracious host, Grant escorted the detectives to their car, while the Laskey's ladies went up stairs together. After only a few steps from the front door, standing on the hot sidewalk and under the blazing sun, Grant firmly stated, "I wanted to walk the two of you outside to let you know my daughter is very fragile; she cannot withstand all the drama of a trial, but the final decision will be hers. Although, I don't understand why you are here to talk about what Thomas did to her, aren't you suppose to be investigating his murder, not a rape? Are the two cases linked together? If that's true, will you please leave my daughter out of it? She didn't kill him and we're trying to move on with our lives, particularly Amy. As a family, we can do without public scandal in our private home life."

Before going inside Grant made one last comment, "I could care less about who killed that no good rapist, who was suppose to be my brother; a brother I once loved, and trusted, but now I love the fact he is dead, and none too soon. That good for nothing jerk, raped my baby for years, and did the same thing to our sister. I haven't had any feeling, or anything else for Thomas, not even a bullet, or a noose! Now....like I wanted to say earlier, but didn't get a chance, you two have a wonderful rest of your lives, but never in this home again." Immediately turning, dismissing the detectives from his presence, he vanished behind closed door, leaving them forever in his rearview mirror of life.

Looking at one another with surprise, question marks written on their face, Holmes said out loud, "may the heavens have mercy on Thomas, and the evil he brought against so many innocent people. Now, let's get out of this heat, go to the mall and grab a bottle of loving essence; afterwards, get something to eat, I'm hungry." The two detectives got in the car, and drove away, while Grant looked out the window watching their every move.

CHAPTER FOURTEEN

Within the following days, the detectives found themselves headed out of town to interview Linda Lane and Kelly Vines. Fortunately for them the two female soldiers were stationed on bases in cities not far apart in distance. Once the duo crossed the state line of Virginia making their way to the military bases, the first person they visited was the once, Corporal Kelly Vines. However, after contacting her, everyone agreed her office was not the best place to hold conversations; quickly deciding to hold their meeting at her apartment after she arrives home.

Time lapsed in slow drizzles after enjoying a great lunch, and discussions of strategy while waiting on Sergeant Vines to finish her day of duties. Finally, around four o'clock in the evening, Vines gave Holmes a phone call, announcing her arrival in less than ten minutes.

Pulling up at the address given to them, they were surprised to find her standing on the stoop waving; presenting a smile of appreciation. Walking onto the street to meet them as they got out of the vehicle, she received them kindly with a warm greeting, "Hello detectives, it's good to finally meet the two of you. Tell me, how was your road trip, and what can I do to help put the untouchable away?" a name she had angrily given Thomas. Quickly Jemison stated, "first, allow us to thank you Sergeant for this meeting after a long day of work. Secondly, we'll appreciate anything that will help in our investigation."

"No thanks necessary. I'll be glad to help, particularly since you have finally started to look into the background of a man that reeked so much havoc in the lives of so many people. His time is up!" Looking with disappointment etched across their faces, Jemison said, "please, can we take this inside?" Shaken by this response, the gleam in Kelly's eyes went out like a smothered candlewick. Saying nothing else, her body language began to slump as she lead the way for the detectives to enter her home. In a sadden tone she offered both something to drink; closing the door behind them. Jemison, responding for both saying, "thanks, but we just finished eating not long ago, but we appreciate you for thinking to ask." Realizing she was not representing her upbringing, Kelly said, "where are my manners? Make yourselves comfortable, have a seat," still sounding as if her world had been crushed. Sitting in the chair in the corner of the room, Kelly took the best seat in the room, yielding her a view of both detectives without having to turn her head, or maneuver her body at any time.

Once everyone was seated comfortably, Jemison began the conversation in her professional, no non-sense tone. Let's start from the beginning, I'm Detective Madison Jemison, and this is my partner Detective Kendrick Holmes and we thank you for allowing us this visit. Now if you can, please tell us the last time you heard, saw, or learned anything about General Laskey?" Purposely, Kelly spoke in the same tone as Jemison, but a bit colder, and callous.

"I don't know why you would ask me such a thing, but I will answer you the best I can. I have not seen, spoken, heard, or looked for anything pertaining to the man who is not worthy to wear the uniform of a soldier, or salute the American flag. The only thing he is worthy of, is a nine by ten jail cell with no windows, or sun light for the rest of his worthless life. But if I see him again; (pausing) to tell you the truth, I will be the one disgracing the uniform we pledged to honor. In the end I will definitely be the one needing those same accommodations I desire for him."

Amused, Holmes yielded a slight smile as he lowered his head.

"Kelly the reason we're here, we have news concerning General Laskey," Jemison stated in a much kinder tone. "Well, if you're not going to tell me the Army's has finally listened to someone about his foul behavior, he has been caught in the act, or they're ready to French fry his behind, then save your news!" She demanded.

"I'm sorry to tell you; the Army is still slothful in doing anything against the General and his conduct," interrupting Jemison's delivery, Kelly stood up from her chair, declaring in a strong voice, "if that's all, you two surely came a long way for nothing! Now if you will excuse me, I think I need to take a shower behind this less than desirable discussion: it has left me feeling unclean! The same way I felt on the night I was attacked on the useless military, non-caring base of Fort Peeks."

"Before you dismiss us, please have a seat so you can listen, and hear all of what we have to say....please."

Cooperating, she took her seat again in order to hear, but wasn't really ready to listen to the detectives empty rhetoric; she remained silent.

"Right before you interrupted me, I was trying to tell you that the military has not taken any actions against the General, but allowed us to continue with our investigation after new evidence was presented. Evidence we believe can prove all the things you, and other ladies have accused him of doing is true. There so much evidence, it has caused the FBI to willing form a task force to work closely with us."

"New evidence! Her eyes lighting up like a Christmas tree and a smile gracing her face like a brilliant, beautiful ornament, when she screamed, "what new evidence? Is it enough to put his behind away for good, and throw away the key?! she asked with excitement."

"Well that won't be necessary."

"Why wouldn't it be necessary?" Kelly anxiously asked.

"It won't be necessary, because General Laskey was found dead."

"Dead? How? Was it of a natural cause? If he died of a natural cause, it's not justice, it's criminal! Now, if his latest victim gutted his behind, that would be better than justice, that would be the best crime in history, a crime no one should be penalized for!" she cheered.

"He was murdered," Holmes vocalized.

Pausing for a few seconds before releasing her next statement, she finally said, "Before we go any further let me ask this....did you come here to tell me about the new evidence, or did you come here to find out where I was on the day of his murder, and if I kill the untouchable jerk? Before you answer these questions, tell me why are you wasting the tax payer dollars, trying to solve his murder? He deserved whatever the killer offered, plus more!"

"Unfortunately, we have to ask questions about your timeline; needless to say, every family deserves to know what happened to their love one," Holmes answered.

"I believe his own family rejoiced behind his death. Anyway, if I had killed the S.O.B, I would gladly tell you, and gladly serve the time, because of what he did to me. Yes, go ahead, check my time log whenever; however you like without revealing me the date, time, place, or how the crime was committed, I have nothing to hide. However, I will say this on my behalf, for the last few years I hardly left the base unless accompanied by many comrades, but if the timeline of my whereabouts is hard to verify, arrest me! because hallelujah!! I'll do the time for the hero who got rid of his broke down, dead behind!" At this point, even straight laced Jemison had to chuckle.

Time ticked quickly from the clock, as the lengthy interview played out, mostly lead by the light hearted Kelly, who shared every detail of the torturous night with the General, and where she was on the night in question.

Uninhibited, by the end of their visit, she asked; making a pledge to the detectives, "when there is a trial concerning his murder, will you let me know? because, I want to be there front, and center to hear every word said by all witnesses. On the other hand, if I am the one standing trial, you won't have to get in touch with me I'll already be there. Either way I want to be present."

Soon the duo left Kelly behind, highly convinced the lady of honor had nothing to do with Thomas demise, and quite sure they would see her again as they responded to her wave of goodbye.

Spending the night in Virginia, the detectives decided to get a good night's rest before interviewing, First Sergeant Lane the next day.

Early the next morning around eight fifty-five, arriving five minutes ahead of schedule at the quaint cottage where Linda lived, they were ushered inside by the hostess with a warm, red carpet welcome, of gracious hospitality. Like their past visits (other than Kandi), the officers believed nothing but the truth would be revealed to them. After sitting down, Linda cheerfully ask, "well detectives, what brings you two all the way to a state so far from home just to see me of all people?"

"Not just for you," Jemison replied, "we also came for other reasons, so let's get straight to the point. We came here today to discuss General Thomas Laskey with you."

Brenda M. Files

"About raping me, or his untimely death?" Surprising both detectives with her response, Jemison quickly shook it off asking, "you already knew Thomas has died?"

"Do you mean murdered? Yes I know. Over the years I have buzzed around, keeping tabs on his worthless behind, like a bee making a honeycomb. I've also monitored that low life side kick of his, the other person that should have been murdered. I guess you came here to find out where I was on the day someone decided to get even with his nasty behind. I'll be glad to fill you in on my activity. I was admitted into the hospital for an emergency appendectomy; down four weeks recovering. Although I left from under his command, the thought of murder became nourishment for my mind, feeding me daily with protein of how to be in two places at one time? Disappointment is now my friend, because I was also hoping someone would rape his nasty behind in prison. Him being rape was a pleasing thought, an appetizer, a sweet dessert of justice, but unfortunately someone took this fantasy, a dream away from me."

"Sorry to hear you had to have surgery Linda, but understand, we will still have to check out your story," Holmes sadly quoted; knowing she was guiltless.

"Be my guest! I wouldn't have it any other way. By the way, what's happening with his co-conspirator who assisted him in raping me? Did she get off scot free, or do I have to continue preparing, and feasting on the idea of how to be in two places at one time?!" spewing out her words without flinching, or a hint of a smile. "We have new evidence that will support the story you shared with your Command Sergeant Major, Charles Mallory. It seems as if she will have a lot of explaining to do. Besides, the FBI has teamed up with us on our investigations, and if found guilty, going scot free will be the last thing she'll do. She will be prosecuted to the fullest," Jemison intervened.

Just like Kelly, Linda's eyes lit up like bright lights of decoration, and her lips gave full demand to be separated, grant the biggest smile she could create to display her beautiful white teeth. At the same time, she held her fists in the air, well above her head like a cheerleader, shaking them vigorously back, and forth in celebration of victory.

For the next few minutes they watched her soundless cheers, creative dances, and tears of joy streamed down her golden skin; almost able to feel her joy. Finally, when the detective left, Linda believed peace would come and find her, bringing along a good night sleep.

In the meantime back home chaos was being stirred up. Kandi had begun reeking extreme havoc on everyone coming against her, and the legacy of Thomas. On the morning the detectives was visiting with Linda, Kandi had gone to the hospital for an unexpectedly visit; opening the door to Charles room, she found me seated, leaning on the bed railing, hands clasped, eyes closed; praying. However, when I heard the crackling of the door separating from its frame, my eyes opened, and surprisingly there stood Kandi. Rising from the chair, I swiftly walked over to where she was standing and without a moment in delay demanded an answer. "What are you doing here?!"

"Well sir! You mean to tell me there is not even a hello for your mother?" Starring at him with a sinister look on her face, along with a wicked grin, she continued. "I am here for the same reason you are, to see Charles who was once my husband, and still is the father of my children. Besides, no one is sharing with me about his condition, so I decided to find out for myself. Is this okay with you?" she vehemently asked.

Brenda M. Files

"No it is not, and neither would it be okay with my dad; a dad I know is mine. You have some nerves coming here uninvited to see someone you know you don't care anything for, or give a rats behind about his well being," clinching my teeth as I spoke in a low tone.

Astounded by his aggressive behavior, Kandi became belligerent, and defiant in her actions, while increasing the volume of her words against her son. "What in the hell do you mean a dad you know is yours?" Shocked, but highly angered by his statement, she pushed her way into the room; closing the door behind her.

Standing in my face within an inch of rubbing noses, our war of words continued. "Just what I said! I am his child. Now if you like, you can call me a liar without a problem; I'll withstand being corrected. But before you call me a liar answer this, are all the children my father raised in our home with you, biologically his?"

"How dare you question me on what your father, and I did in our home, while raising our children?"

"I'm not questioning what he did, I'm questioning what you did! You see I know, and believe my father never brought an outside child home from some other home, or hospital for you to raise after creating them with someone else; he was too busy thinking he was producing all of his children with you. From what I remember as the oldest child, all the children that were brought into our home came from the hospital in your arms, and the man laying in that hospital bed, walked in the house alongside you. The same man who still considers my sister, and brother his children. Again, when ready, you can call me a liar."

"If you want the truth, I surely hope you can handle it when its delivered," still smiling wickedly. With her hands on her hips, head tilted to one side, Kandi positioned herself for combat; ready to attack. At the same time, I deliberately refused to offer, or suggest having a seat, "Kandi, you'll be surprised at what I can handle."

"Well, let me tell you about the real deal. Let me tell you the truth about what you say you want to hear; surly something daddy dearest failed to do. In the beginning we had goals, aspirations, but your father somehow put us in a hell hole of a situation when we joined the military. Everything fell apart, because he wouldn't finish his education, which caused us to join under false pretense in order to fulfill lifelong dreams of becoming officers. Little did I know at the time, we were committing treasonous crimes that would bring dishonorably discharges, prison, or both."

At this point, I knew telling the whole truth was a character flaw of Kandi, the same as never taking ownership of her wrong doing, but I listened anyway. "After learning about all of the illegality surrounding us, your father came up with another grand scheme of dishonesty with the army, he decided we would live a life of being single. Silly, and in love, I went along with this plan of fraud. If I had too, I'd to do it all over again, and wouldn't change a thing, because the army life has not only been good to me and your father, but extended great lives for our children. Although, from the sound, and look of things, there is a lot of ungratefulness running deep in this family. Nevertheless, time began to erode the relationship between us, because of poor choices, and hidden secrets in the basement of our crooked lives. Assuming full responsibility as mother and father, I found no time, or desire to visit his home to play footsie under the sheets with your father at the end of the day just to satisfy his manly desires, and selfishly made the decision to begin an outside affair after years of separation to deal with loneliness. I was prompted to do the same. Eventually I fell in love with someone else, producing two beautiful children, but for some reason I'm sure you already know this! Like I'm also sure you already know who fathered Diamond and Terrence, children made in pure love. Even with all the efforts of brainwashing Terrence against me, you nor your father's words of poison can penetrate the mind of my Diamond; she is tough, just like her name. Sadly for me, those times I had to bring them home in my arms with your father walking alongside me, I was doing what was necessary to protect our family's name, and honor, because their true father was committed to another."

"Honor," I declared, no longer able to remain silent. "How is it honor when you lie? Tell me, why would you being separated from a man and too tired to play footsie, or satisfy his manly desires, be deceitful enough to have him in your bed when you found yourself pregnant with another man's children? And please tell me why would you make your way to his bed to give him false hope, give him pleasure just to use him in the pretense of making babies you knew he wanted, but they had already conceived?! Or did you think after not being with you, a brilliant man like my father, was dumb enough to believe in immaculate conceptions, and not formulate the legitimacy of my sister and brother? Unless you are telling me that God spoke to him in a dream as a just man, telling him not to be afraid, because the children Kandi is carrying, are holy one's! But before you lie on God, answer this for me please...do you think I'm that dumb?" I could tell a nerve had been struck; inwardly she was smoking like a tank of liquid nitrogen, ready to release cold, flesh burning steam. Satisfied, these questions disrupted her moments of basking in self glory, brought leaps of joy into my heart.

"Junior you are so disrespectful! You're no better than the disfigured cloth you are cut from," she blared forcefully toward me.

"Careful! Remember, the cloth can be cut both ways; the side you're speaking of, could be your half."

"I could never produce, or teach such disrespectful insolence."

"Again, be careful! Remember, having an affair, and producing outside children while married is insolent, and disrespectful, or will you call Webster's definition a lie? If you prove Webster wrong, I can stand being corrected."

Suddenly in the background, I heard my father make a slight groaning sound, quickly turning to see if my ears were correct, I saw his fingers moving, and without delay said to the woman in the room, "you will have to leave now," while grabbing her upper arm to help in exiting through the now, open door.

"No! I will stay with him while you get the nurse, and doctor," she insisted.

"No hell you won't! I don't trust you alone with my father. You can stay inside this hospital because this is a public facility, but you most certainly have to get out of this room!" I demanded while pushing her out the door. Controlling her tempo, holding onto her arm, I continued leading her in a swift trek to the nurse's station.

Once we arrived at the destination, I loosened my grip, giving her a slight shove to help her continue moving forward. At this point, I did not care if I left any physical bruising on her body, while setting off alarms about what was happening in my father's room. "Nurse, please come quickly, my father made a sound, he moved his fingers!"

Immediately, two of the nurse leaped from their chairs, and began running down the corridor while another nurse picked up the phone, called the operator, so the doctors on duty could be alerted to come to his room. Hanging up the phone she said, "please stay here, or stand outside your father's door Mr. Charles until the doctor's finish examining him, afterwards someone will come out to speak with you."

I don't remember responding; by that time thunderous footsteps could be heard roaring throughout the corridor, then out of nowhere doctors appeared racing down the hall toward his room, all dressed in green scrubs, covered by white lab coats. Never once did they cease their stride, until they opened the door for their entrance, hurriedly closing it behind them. Standing alone with my mother, caused me to cringe. Knowing she had not dismissed herself from my presence; the conversation previously held between us had grown far too old, I asked in a strained tone,

"Lady, why are you still here? In case you forgot, my father's well being does not concern you any longer!"

"How dare you say that? I will always have concerns for his well being, and the feelings of my children," trying to sound sorrowful.

"For which set of children do you concern yourself about? If it's my father's set, why haven't you gone to the jailhouse to visit Terence?"

"You just contradicted, and made your point invalid, because Terrence is from the seed of Thomas," sounding smug.

"No, I just validated my point! You see....Thomas may have planted the seed to produce Terrence, but it took a real man like Charles Sr. to raise, and be the dad he needed. In the end Terrance is from the same set of children as the one standing before. We were all produced through the love of our dad. So I'll ask again, why are you here?!"

In a split second, she turned away from me without saying another word; angrily heading toward the elevators. Looking at her backside, I smiled with sheer delight; thanking God, because He knew I had had enough. Pacing back, and forth throughout the hallways for over thirty minutes, which seemed like an eternity, finally one of the attending physicians came out to announce; my father had come out of his comma. Being grateful, I thanked God for my mother and her contribution, because the disturbing sound of her voice helped to bring him back to us.

Later, furious about the things that transpired between the two of us, our mother found herself waiting to visit Terrence at the county jail, where she was escorted to the visiting area to be seated on a stool, in front of a large pane of glass. Anxiously, Terrance sat down also, allowing no time to escape before picking up the telephone receiver planted on the wall; Kandi followed suit. Pressing the phone firmly against their ear, she began to sorely announce in a voice of judgment and disapproval, "Tell me Terrence, why did you kill Thomas? How could you hurt me like this?! You knew how much I loved him! But I guess no one wants to see me happy! Is this the reason you took him from me, because you all don't want to see me happy unless it's with Charles, someone I don't love? Please tell me, why would my children want unhappiness and misery in my life?"

Suddenly the pleasing, joyous feeling dancing inside his entire body died, erasing happiness from his face. Terrence having the capability to speak, but at that moment was reluctant to release any words; fearing what would come out. Instead he permitted her to continue with wild accusation. Soon, beginning not to care, he shook off the bridle, in order to blast her with all powers from his tongue. "You've brought yourself here where I am fighting for my life, held for something someone else has done, and have the audacity to sit there accusing me with conjectures; no proof! What gives you the right?! Lady...I want you to listen, and listen well! I have no idea what you feel for anyone, including that poor example of a man, who was a good for nothing rapist you proclaim to love! I wouldn't waste my time trying to figure you out, and I don't care if you hurt for the rest of your life! I don't care if you ever had, or will have happiness! You are not important among my concerns, or cares! I have things more pressing in my life; people more relevant! Just in case you haven't noticed, I am locked behind steel bars, divided from the world by a bullet proof glass! A glass that stands between me, and all my welcomed guest; my true family who loves me! A glass between me, and people who want to embrace and believe in me, but as far as caring about your pain, or happiness, it's dead to me, just like you are......MOTHER! Now, if you will please excuse me, find your own way to the door of which you came, because right now it would be impossible for me to escort you out; since I don't know where the front door is located!"

Getting up from the hard metal stool, he turned quickly away from his mother, but before he could call for the guard, she banged on the thick glass several times with the receiver of the phone, screaming unclear words. Twirling around, he saw someone no longer looking like his mother, but a person deranged, lacking the presence of foam drooling from the corner of her mouth. Jerking the phone from its base once again, he placed it against his ear to listen to her narcissistic ranting. "Don't you dare walk away from me, I am your mother! I'm tired of the disloyalty, and disrespect shown, after all of the sacrifices I have made. I know we are both overcome by the pain beyond our control, but as family banding together, we can overcome, and withstand anything headed our way."

"Overcome, band, withstand, family, you are one bold, delusional person! There has not been a you, with us in a very long time! Plus I don't think these words will be connect with us again!" Terrance strongly stated.

"Why do you have to be so negative?

"Why did you have to be so negative when you first arrived here? First of all you started off accusing me, finding me guilty before a trial could stand a chance of vindicating me from this horrible injustice of wrong. Secondly, you were correct when you said we are both overcome by pain, but decided to increase mine when you charged me with allegations of not wanting you to have happiness. Go, and be happy! But for you to think we want you with our father is a joke that's on you; contrary to belief, he wouldn't have anything to do with you...period! Most importantly, his children will not, even if he wanted to allow hell to re-enter into his life. Now that I have you here, will you please tell me the truth if you know how?! who in hell is my biological daddy, because I'm sure that's where he's from?!" bulging his eyes as he asked this very vital question.

No longer having children doting over her, or cradling her feeling, she became engaged with rage. Standing up from the uncomfortable metal stool, she picked up her purse, while saying to Terence before hanging up the phone, "you don't have a daddy, or a mother! You can just stay in here and rot in this miserable hole, a place where all murderers belong! I pray they throw away the key so you'll never have a way out of here, except in death, that way you will never have to find your way to the front door!" Before she could place the phone on the hook, he managed to say, "Watch what you pray for, because the place you prepare for me in a miserable hole, may be the same place you'll rot, leaving you to never find an exit!"

Slamming down the phone, she quickly turned away, calling for the guards to let her out of the small visiting area. While waiting on the attendee to answer her call, Terrence wanted desperately for her to turn around to see him waving goodbye, while mouthing slowly, words that couldn't be heard, 'never come back! Unfortunately, she never turned around to look at him.

CHAPTER FIFTEEN

Two days later, I found Terrence to be in good spirits during our visit as he began sharing with me the short, but unimaginable time he spent with our mother.

Meanwhile, after finding out dad was recovering, she began calling constantly asking about his memory, and speech development. This overwhelming concern for the man we love, caused chilling disturbance to rush through me, until Taylor discovered some interesting information left by her mother; securely storing its existence.

Taylor's mother had hired a private investigator, by the name of Sam Smith, (but never mentioning his name in her documents) to keep a close watch on her husband; a person Taylor readily contacted. Sam a tall, slim, unshaven, gruff, man with a swollen and extended belly, who loved Peggy.

Weeks after the ex-policeman had been following Thomas day and night, documenting many pictures and keeping intricate, detailed notes, he hated disclosing these things with Peggy; things that left her flabbergasted.

Once Sam learned of all the no good things Thomas, and Kandi had done to so many people, he continued to collect evidence on them, even when he no longer had a living client. Peggy was not only a smart woman, but also very aware, her life was in danger.

With determination to follow every instructions to the letter, committed to telling Peggy's truth, Sam knew it was time to contact and share all information with Taylor; he also included me, per Taylor's request. From the moment the story started to unfold, we knew we had hit jack pot. Sam gave all information to us at no cost, because he believed Peggy had paid in full with her life. Fortunately for us; according to Sam, he followed Thomas to my father's home on the day he was shot. After watching him knock on the door, and to his surprise my father allowed him to come inside, causing intrigue to peak his interest more.

At this point, Sam decided to use his high tech, supersonic, audio recorder listening devise to capture the entire conversation, held between my father and Thomas. Carefully listening to everything while gathering evidence, he even recorded the solemn greetings.

Immediately after Thomas entered into the home, an argument started to brew among the two gentlemen.

"Charles, I want you to turn over to me all the papers Peggy unlawfully gave to you."

"Listen Thomas, whatever you think Peggy may have given me, or think I may have is none of your business. Now if there is nothing else I can do for you, please leave my home."

"I am not leaving here until I have what I came for. Remember, I am your commanding officer, and if you deliberately disobey my order I can bring charges against you, and have you court martial! what you and Peggy have done is known as stealing! Trust me, it doesn't matter you're retired, you can still be punished for this kind of behavior. Is this what you want?" he arrogantly asked.

"The question should be, is this what you want?"

"I told you what I want! and I want it now, you worthless piece of s..."

Interrupting him, Charles shouted, "Do you really think you can bring your sick, warped behind into the privacy of my home making demands of me, and think I would comply?! You have disrupted our family life since the day we met! Well, today I'm here to tell you the line has been drawn in the sand where you are concerned, so bring your charges against me, I am ready to face the consequences! I'm ready to take ownership of my wrong doings! Are you?"

"I have no consequences to face, I have no wrong doings to take ownership of; even if I did who would believe you against me. I am a high ranking General in the United Stated Army, leaving you with the inability to touch me; you are a nobody! So if you think, whatever my wife gave you will implicate me in any crimes, will only bring you heartaches. It will also disfigure Peggy's name, even in death. Please, go ahead, you have my permission to turn over false documents, so I can have you disgraced."

"Thanks for your permission! I think I will. Whether these documents can prove you killed Peggy or not, they will prove you raped Janice Brooks, Linda Lane and Kelly Vines. Hell man, they will prove you raped your own sister, niece, and daughter! And what's making me so angry right now, besides the fact I want to kill your behind, but thank God I'm not a criminal like you...it can prove you kidnapped, and raped my child twice. Worst of all; what really makes this whole thing so sickening, you drew Kandi into your evil, distorted, world of corruption. Unfortunately, I can't place the entire blame on you for her participation; she is a grown woman, who definitely has a mind of her own. Kandi could have at anytime, walked away, turned your behind in to the police, but she chose not to do so, making both of you warped, and should suffer whatever consequences is handed down: hopefully it will be, putting both of you to death."

Angered, Thomas hands began trembling while raising his voice in rebellion.

"You can't prove anything behind words written by a distraught, jealous and suicidal woman during a mental, downward spiral!"

"You are probably right about her being emotionally distraught, but contrary to your belief, our claim can be proven through evidence you have provided."

"I have never given you, or Peggy anything that would consist of a crime against me!"

"You're right, not a crime, but many crimes. Even though you always thought you were smarter than everyone else, Peggy was, and always have been one step ahead in everything you tried to do. You should have given her more credit. One day while you were on a business trip, she found the underground railroad to your sexual stash, consisting of recordings and many hand written documents detailing, rape, sodomy, and other crimes. Thank goodness, all were well recorded by none other than.....you."

Speechless, Thomas stood there motionless for what seemed like forever, permitting time for his head to start pounding; tightening as if it had been placed in the jaws of a large metal vise, creating pressure well beyond his ability to tolerate. Looking in the face of evil, knowing a grand explosion was about to happen, Charles prepared himself for anything his unwelcomed guest would say, or do during this stressful, out of control moment. Finally, Thomas responded, "How dare you steal from me!"

"Steal from you!" I have never taken anything from anyone that wasn't mine throughout my entire life time, not even another man's wife. What I have in my possession are document given to me by a fine, very creditable lady, who was your wife."

"She also had no right to steal from me! By law, you received stolen goods."

"I received goods from Peggy, filled with information containing nothing less than the crimes of murders, and high treason, so trust me when say....I may go to jail for obstruction of justice, also court martial for fraternization, but I can surely guarantee one thing, you and Kandi will be right behind me for the same charges, and so much more. I also believe you will be found guilty of Peggy's murder, not a suicide. Now Mr. intruder, will you leave my home?"

"I'll tell you one more time, after that I'll gladly leave! Give me my property!"

"There is nothing here that belongs to you; even if there was, I will only give it to the proper authority, which you are not."

Suddenly Charles moved past where Thomas stood to extend an invitational of a goodbye from his annoying presence, by opening up the front door. Regrettably, this was the last thing my father would remember about that day. Alarmed, Thomas grabbed a large wooden statue my father purchased while visiting Africa, and struck him over his head. Pleased, he stood over his unconscious body feeling gratified, saying in a disturbing, cynical tone, "You should have given me what I wanted, now you'll pay!" From his pocket, he pulled out a handkerchief; a pair of rubber gloves to cover his hands for protection; wiping away any possible evidence with the handkerchief, he placed the figurine back in its original position, neatly inserted the cloth in his pocket, (now redesigned with Charles blood) and began tending to the unconscious victim. Profusely sweating in his struggling efforts to move Charles into the bedroom, Thomas finally managed to lift his motionless, but still very much alive, body onto the bed. Allowing his back to fall onto the mattress, leaving his feet planted on the floor; breathing heavily, Thomas pulled the gun he brought with him from the band of his trousers, placed the weapon inside Charles hand, covered the nozzle with a pillow, placed the victims right index finger on the trigger, pressed the weapon against his temple, forced the unaware person to pull the trigger; until a bullet was released from the chamber, into the head of his victim. Calculating, Thomas left the gun on the bed next to the seemingly lifeless body to solidify a suicide. Hastily he rummaged through the entire house looking for documents, photos and recording that were not there: everything had been placed in a safety deposit box.

Unsuccessful in the mission of finding what he came for, but found a gun in the nightstand next to the bed, he took the weapon out of the drawer, and in his diabolical thinking, replaced the gun he brought with the one he believed belonged to be the victim. Taking Charles hand, he wrapped it around the gun's handle in order to transfer prints, and gunpowder residue onto the weapon; again creating a believable suicide. Finished, Thomas decided to take the handkerchief and rubber gloves with him, leaving behind Charles body in a position staged for someone else to eventually find. Stricken with panic, believing the noise of gunfire may have been heard by someone in the quiet, quaint neighborhood, he hurriedly ran out of the house. However, the sound had already traveled, reaching the waiting ears of Sam's equipment, a man of the law. Startled by the noise, but hesitant to leave the surveillance point, he remained seated. However, he didn't have to wait very long before Thomas appeared from around the backside of the home carrying a plastic garbage bag, something he didn't have when he arrived, Walking swiftly down the walkway, then onto the street to reach his car where he parked earlier, got inside as if nothing happened, he quickly drove away: down the backstreet of a dark, wicked mind, feeling well pleased. Sam gracefully began sharing everything with us. "Within seconds of his departure, I exited my van, but not before regaining my composure. Casually strolling toward the house to see if I could locate what had taken place inside of the home; looking around I slowly moved forward to make sure there were no on lookers standing around trying to investigate the sound of gunfire. Seeing there were no inquiring minds lurking, I continued searching; thinking, 'I should have followed that low down coward to find out what was in that plastic bag, and what he was going to do with it?' Whatever it was, I knew it wouldn't be in existence much longer.

Bringing my train of thought back into focus, I walked around the parameter of the house searching for any unlocked entrance, but found all doors securely locked. Learning I couldn't obtain access into the house through the doors, I moved from window to window hoping to find a small opening to gather a view of what may have taken place, and find Charles. A few seconds later, but not a surprise, my eyes caught a glimpse of him through a small division in the curtains: his upper body was laying backwards on the bed, bleeding profusely from what seemed to be a wound to the head area. After seeing the pistol laying next to his motionless body, I assumed he was dead.

Without haste, I rushed back to my vehicle, jumped inside, turned on the engine, and placed the van in the gear of drive. Remembering my promise to Peggy, I called the police as a concerned citizen from a untraceable phone number, reporting the sound of shots fired, giving them Charles address as the central location, and soon drove away just like Thomas. Sadly, the police found nothing suspicious, or out of order when they arrived, after giving a quick search of the area; leaving the scene without further actions.

Brenda M. Files

Later, I learned you found his body the following morning. This discovery helped me to feel much better, but not my best, until I spoke with you, and Taylor in person to tell you how very sorrowful I am. The day I left your father for dead was one of the worst time for me in all of the forty years I've worked in law enforcement. I can't apologize enough for my actions of being a coward. I just didn't want to lose focus, or involve the police in my case until I was ready. Will you please forgive me?"

Smiling at the tall, lanky man with the extended, swollen belly and un-kept hair, I pleasingly stated, "You are a person never to feel bad about your work. Hold pride for the things you've done. You had a job, and a terrible decision to make, and as far as I'm concerned, you made a good one. You saved my dad's reputation from a lifetime of scandal, possibly prison; by capturing the truth on tape, and many photographs taken. Sam, you saved all of our lives, so thank you."

"I appreciate your kindness, but I can't take credit not owed to me. The thanks belong to one of the finest, most beautiful ladies God created to walk this earth. A lady who never wore a hero's cape, or given a medal; her name is Peggy Laskey." Turning his attention to Taylor, Sam said, "your mother was the best client I've ever worked for, and all I could ever bring to her was heartache. I want you to know young lady, until the trail finally end, and justice is served....like I promised your mother, this case will always have my full attention."

Standing up from the chair, Sam walked across the room with his hands in his pockets, when suddenly he said, "one day your mother gave me permission to come into her home while Thomas was at work; allowing me free hands to place listening, and camera devices throughout the home, due to lingering trust issues against him. Like I said before, she was a very smart lady. On one particular evening after a long day at work, no children greeting her any longer, Peggy arrived home exhausted; falling asleep on the sofa: a short while later you could hear the sound of tumbling locks from the entrance door being manipulated; soon the crackling sounds of its opening, permitted Thomas to walk inside. Looking at her lying on the sofa, he became arrogant: however, at this point I will allow you to hear and see for yourselves," pushing play on the recorder, he remained silent.

"Every time I see, or look at you, you're in the same place. Either let the lie your daughter told go, a lie causing all these degrees of separation, or get the hell out of my house. Trust me, I am sick of looking at you."

"You are a low down, good for nothing SOB Thomas! One day you will get yours, and it may come sooner than you think."

"You know no one can touch me! I am a high ranking, respected General in command of an entire Army base, overseeing hundreds of soldiers, admired by many, making me too high to touch. I am just as high as any president, or senators of the United States of America; even higher! And no matter what you, or Charles think you can say to destroy me, it will not hold water against my honorable name."

"You are so arrogant and very much misinformed. No one is untouchable! No one is so high, not even a president, that can't be brought down. For your sake, don't go too far up in self lifting if you don't want to crash, and burn when landing back to earth."

"Crash and burn is what you do; don't compare my great worth in society to your almost non-existent life. The only reason people know you are alive; I made you visible, otherwise you blend into a blacken background."

"Like I said, you'll get yours. You should have gotten it a long time ago when your sister mysteriously died."

Silence fell throughout the room, causing Thomas to become disturbed by her aggressive and accusatory tone. Immediately seeing evil growing rapidly in his eyes; his jaws bones flexing up and down, Peggy could hear the sound of gritting teeth; knowing instantly he was no longer Thomas. Permitting himself to reply, he shared with her in a ice cold, vicious tone, many graphic details,

"You have always believed I had something to do with her death. Well, since we're on the subject of belief about death, allow me to thoroughly inform you. Yes, I molested my sister for years, I also did the same thing to a couple of our young female neighbors; daring them to talk. After Grant found me with our sister, I convince his dumb behind I was getting help for my out of control sexual problem; without doubt, he believed me.

Over time she learned how to find enjoyment in our convenient arrangement, because in the end it was all about satisfying me, particularly when she became more afraid of me, instead of finding comfort in the threats made against me by Grant. This is why she decided to relax and enjoy: until the day she decided to become aggressive with newly, over developed nerves without my permission. She was trying to come from under years of my control, making ridiculous demands; this was the wrong idea for her to give birth too. Once I heard her plans of telling Grant, and the entire family as I began mounting her for an evening of fun filled pleasure, I found my hands completely covering; penetrating her throat. In the next moment without thought, I started squeezing tighter, and tighter until she stopped

Saluting Madness   181

kicking, squirming, and breathing. This was an act I found to be the ultimate in pleasure, more than any sexual act I could ever encounter."

Astonished; frighten by this revelation of details about his sister's murder, Peggy said nothing as she listened to the insanity that was flowing from his mouth, until a burning question couldn't take the bragging any longer.

"What kind of monster could do such a thing to their sister?"

"Hold on! you don't have to be a monster to do it when you have great needs, and desires to be fulfilled."

"A desire to rape, and kill is what an insane person would think is fulfilling? You really are a monster."

"I couldn't be much of a monster, because you were more than happy when I asked for your hand in marriage. You answered yes before I completed the question, not to mention how much you enjoyed being in my bed. So when you call me a monster, I won't take offense."

The sound of nervousness rose in Peggy's voice and her fear grew rapidly. Overpowered by an overwhelming desire to hear all of the deeds done to others spew from his wicked mouth, she ingested every morsel of craziness his tone released, while he celebrated his violent conquests.

"You should be offended, but that would make you a human with a heart, things you lack being, or having."

"Again, you must have thought I was a human with a heart when you married, and stayed with me all these years. Oops, I'm so sorry, I didn't mean to keep you entertained by going on-and-on about what your desires are for me; we were talking about Jean, and what she wanted.

Now, where were we? Oh yes! Looking down on her lifeless body smiling, after finishing what I started before I strangled her, I got one of her personal scarves from the vanity drawer, placed it around her neck to set her up for an apparent suicide. During my next step, I was surprised she was heavy being so small, making her not as easily managed as I thought. Jumping on the bed, I began pulling the other end of the lynching device until her butt started to rise from the floor; with a lot of assertion, eventually her body began to slide upward to finally rest on the back of her heels. Next, I curled the end of the scarf around the bedpost, tied it securely in place and allowed her head to slump forward. Satisfied with the execution of my plan, resulting in unbelievable talent of presentation, I went to the bathroom, retrieved a wet hand towel, came back, wiped away anything that would look suspicious on the lower part of the dead body; put her on fresh panties and threw the other pair away without thought of my own cleanliness. After getting dressed, I left the house only to return much later when enough time had lapsed, and I knew someone else in the family would be responsible for finding her lifeless body. The next day I had to label myself as a genius, because as planned, her death was declared a suicide! I'm Brilliant!"

"How could you Thomas," Peggy asked.

"How could I not. You don't know the thrill until you do something highly, and illegally wrong, not to mention getting away with it. After that day, I have had such a thirst for being in control, a thirst that I'm never able to quench, always needing to be more and more hydrated. By the time Diane Baker decided to bring her selfish trickery, and conniving behind into my life, I was a pro. She knew I was married after finding herself pregnant, but selfishly thought this would control my life. But just like everybody else, she had to fall in line, she had to realize I am the controller of lives."

Saluting Madness   183

Becoming more fearful of the man she once loved, the father of her children, she began contemplating, and looking around for an escape route, plus a weapon to help in her defense to make her exit from danger.

Finally laying eyes on a letter opener they received as a wedding present, it became her weapon of choice. In effort to distract his attention, Peggy ask a question.

"Thomas, please tell me you didn't hurt Diane! If you did, tell me why, because there was really no reason?"

"Sorry! Guilty as charged. Besides I couldn't have her destroying my life, my career, or my marriage for something not yet human, growing inside of her body. The only person I will allow to do that to me, is me. After pleading with her to have an abortion, always receiving refusals, she had to go, never to come back. Unfortunately, her insistence of telling you, left me with no choice but to make you, or Charles look as if you brought harm to Diane; I decided on Charles. I planted crucial information, like blood evidence among his property to help lead police into believing he was the perpetrator! Guess what! It worked! My mind soon grew in peace, until I learned you had given Charles information stolen from my possession that may lead police back to me. I watched everything you did Peggy while I was away on business. I had trusty cameras hidden around the house in very secluded places. That's how I know you made copies of my secrets, and gave this information to Charles."

Looking crossed, evil instantly redesigned his face as he continued speaking. "Now I couldn't have that could I Peggy? Particularly, if he has facts that I raped my own daughter in his possession. You've left me with no choice, but to get rid of you, and Charles nosey behinds!" Suddenly, he leaped up from the chair where he had taken a seat near the front door, blocking her escape plan; grabbing the letter opener from the sofa table, pointing it in the direction of the madman standing in front of her, feeling threaten she immediately went into self- defense mode. Laughing out loud he questioned her action, "please tell me, what are you suppose to do with that, stab yourself?"

"Whatever I have to, including kill you," she declared as sweat ran heavily down her face; her hands shaking, revealing to him, her level of fear. "Well...if you are going to kill me, you need to stop shaking before the letter opener either finds its way inside you, or on the floor. Mrs. Laskey, do you see me shaking? No you do not! because I have the heart, and taste for this kind of excitement. Right now, I can smell the fear, I can also taste the sweat from your brow; can you say the same?"

Moving closer to where she stood, Peggy's life started to flash before her eyes; remembering the joyous time they had as a family in every room of their home, yet at the same time, lowly moved sideways, because it was the only direction left for her to travel. In an instant, his course of movement followed hers. Peggy tried speaking many words of discouragement to loosen all thoughts of harm, but Thomas mind was now programmed for doing evil.

"Please Thomas, you don't want to do whatever it is you're thinking."

"Tell me Peggy.....what am I thinking?!"

"I don't know, but I don't think you have my best interest in mind; if you did I would feel safe."

"Haven't I always taken care of you? Haven't you always been safe?"

"Yes you have, but for some reason I'm not feeling that level of comfort, or safety."

"Well you shouldn't, because now you're not safe!"

Lunging toward her with his arms stretched forward, and fingers curled, he jumped over the coffee table as she turned in effort to flee, sounds of crashing glass onto the floor was the background noise as we clearly saw and heard all the events unfolding against his frighten wife, pleading in grueling anguish. Even though this madness had already taken place, the sound alone made our hearts race in tremendous fear. Suddenly all went silent, and out of view; the only thing heard was Thomas calmly speaking with someone on the other end of the telephone, inviting them to come over. "Unfortunately," Sam stated, "I was out of town for a few days; away from my ears when all of this happened to Peggy; for this, I can never forgive myself." Taylor simply walked over to him, placed her arm around his shoulders and calmly said, "my mother believed in you, and so do we. We know if you had been there, you would have protected her." Sam smiled as we continued viewing the recordings.

Around a half hour later the doorbell rang; allowing the visitor to enter into the house out of camera view. But before he could fully close the door behind the person he began telling his version of what had taken place. Suddenly changing gears, he started doling out instruction of what was expected of the unknown stranger. "I couldn't get her to the car, so I called you to help me dispose of her dead body." Once the voice was revealed, no one was surprised who the accomplice was. "Where is she?" Kandi asked.

"She's in the dining room."

Walking briskly, we could hear shoes traveling across the wooden floors in loud thunderous claps as they entered the room; bringing Kandi clearly into view of the camera. Kneeling down to check her pulse, she was amazingly surprised and quickly rang out in a loud voice, "Thomas, Peggy is still alive!"

Calmly he stated after hearing the revealing news, "I don't care if she's alive, to me she is dead! In the final analysis, she knows too much about our secrets, we can't let her go on living."

"What was said to you to make you believe she knew anything? Did she give you proof?"

Convincing her with lies he said, "she has proof I raped Amy! She also knows how I killed Diane. Worst of it all, she added you in the mix of these crimes."

"I had nothing to do with the murder of Diane!" Her level of speaking beginning to climb in dramatic fear.

"I know! I tried to tell her, but after believing you ruined our marriage, she's more than willing to believe anything negative about you." Frighten of the next answer, but needing to know, Kandi reluctantly asked, "What is it you would have us to do?"

"If we don't want to go to prison for the rest of our lives, we need to get rid of her...permanently."

"Please tell me you're kidding!" She exclaimed.

"Why would I kid about our future, or prison? If she lives we will have major problems with no feasible answer against the evidence she may be able to provide against us. Do we really want to take a chance on losing our freedom, especially since we can't retrieve the information; we don't even have an idea where it could be hidden?

Without hesitation, her heart was completely into whatever he needed, including murder. Frighten, but ready to risk everything for the man she loved, Kandi allowed her life to be completely controlled by Thomas crimes: crimes now known by other people; people who had no love lose for her, or Thomas. His lies would soon leave her with no way out. Swallowing all honor, she looked at him with loving eyes, smiled, then walked over to give him a hug, saying, "Thomas, I am with you no matter what." Immediately he went into cover-up mode, "here's what we will do! I will go to the bathroom, get a pair of gloves for each of us so we don't leave any fingerprints for evidence, but right now I want you to get on her computer, type up a short suicide letter, but remember, never take off your gloves. Once that's done, we'll get her into the trunk of my car after lining it with some duty heavy plastic, then you'll follow me to Longtrail State park; I'll take it from there." Her love for Thomas would not release her from this god forbidden plan, even if she wanted to be free.

Finally, all the blank spaces had been filled in by Sam on how Peggy was led out to Longtrail park where her body was found hanging from that old oak tree, early one frosty morning by two people during their morning jog. Without delay, I began sharing with Taylor and Sam, the gruesome impeccable details I read from Thomas diary of how Peggy really met her demise.

While following his SUV crying, many disturbing thoughts raced through her mind, producing mounting fears and increased hand shaking, especially after the two vehicle finally pulled of the road onto a isolated path. Nevertheless, she stayed on this treacherous course of insanity. Parking the cars side by side, Kandi must have been engrossed in deep personal thoughts; appearing blindsided when Thomas knocked on the driver's side window, causing her to tremble and release a small yelp. Rapidly rolling down the pane of glass to listen to his instructions; trying to wipe the tears from her eyes. "Leave the suicide note on the driver's seat, then help me remove her body from the trunk."

Brenda M. Files

Distraught by the plan of murder, Kandi rolled the window up, exited the vehicle with tears running rampantly down her face, allowed Thomas to lead her to the trunk of the car, opened it, only to reveal Peggy in a battling mode, fighting for her life. Surprised by the alertness of their potential victim, both assailants jumped from temporary fright, but hurriedly went into defensive mode. In great effort, both tried to dodge the vigorous flings of her windmill, whirling arms; hitting Kandi across the face a few times. Becoming highly angered, Thomas aggressively grabbed her protective devices with both of his hands; manhandling the situation with all of his might, he finally locked them together, gaining complete control of her unpredictable motions. Yanking her out of the trunk by her arms and threw her onto the ground; yelling out to Kandi in frustration, "get the rope from the front seat of my the car!"

Overwhelming fear, caused Kandi to remain parked in hesitation until the bellowing of his voice sounded off once again, "move it, I can't hold her much longer!" Not wasting another moment, she quickly retrieved the rope and, hurriedly brought it back to him. Snatching it from her hand, placing it around Peggy's neck, he pulled it tightly, leading her to grabbing hold of the lynching equipment pressed against her throat; pulling desperately to loosen its grip, she vigorously kicked and struggled to set herself free. In the meantime, while listening to Kandi annoying whimpering sounds of panic traveling through the darkness of night, Thomas said nothing.

Finally losing consciousness, Peggy's body went limp, prompting Thomas to demand more assistance. "Kandi, get your act together; help me get her body underneath that branch over there," pointing toward a large oak tree.

Doing as she was told, Kandi picked up Peggy's legs, Thomas handling the upper body; planted her on the ground beneath the tree, threw the other end of the rope across the chosen limb, and without Kandi's help the wicked person began pulling slowly, lifting upwardly, her living body. When Peggy started to feel the sensation around her neck, she awoke from her unconscious state, while clutching the rope around her neck, once again trying without success, to release its hold. Meanwhile, her feet searched to find a piece of earth, a place of comfort for her toes to rest upon; praying not to become airborne.

Soon all efforts were lost as she swirled around, dancing freely in the tree; knowing nothing could help at that point, she struggled until death finally set her free. Thomas tied the end of the rope he held in his hand to a lower limb, securing her in place, and stepped backwards to admire his completed, suicide mission. Looking at Kandi displeased, he said, "Get in the car, I'm driving! And please stop your pretend whimpering!" Silently she rode in the passenger seat, recalling the forged suicide note.

'Dear Taylor and Chandler, my beautiful daughters, I am so sorry to leave you behind, because of weakness and not being able to cope with all of the embarrassing thing going on with our family. I'm sorry for not staying around to be there to protect the two of you when you will need me the most. Please forgive me for my cowardly ways. I wish I had the stamina to continue this journey with the two of you as you transform into the ladies I know you will become; see my grandchildren you will one day produce. Forgive me, and please live your lives to the fullest. Never forget me. I'll always be, your loving mother Peggy.'

In the meantime, Thomas was on an elevated high of satisfaction, insisting on being in the home where Peggy

Brenda M. Files

was murdered and make love in the spot of her death. After fulfilling their desires of sacrilegious acts in the family home, Thomas went into the kitchen; a few moments later, returning with a bottle of wine to celebrate their victory. Holding their glasses high, clanging them together, Thomas made a toast, "to our new life! may we make it the best life ever, solidifying togetherness in our beautiful partnership of indestructible, adventurous, controlling freedom!"

"Hear, hear," Kandi replied in delight, demonstrating no sign of regret, or remorse for the unlawful deed done to Peggy, because Thomas now, belonged to her. A short while later, they found themselves embracing in heated passion once again, fueled by alcohol, celebrating Thomas accomplishment of killing for the thrill; proudly inducting Kandi as his newly found protégé.

CHAPTER SIXTEEN

In days to come, back at the hospital while Peggy's body was being discovered, we had a visit from Detectives Holmes and Jemison, two people who seemed to have concern for my father's well being. Introducing themselves with smiles and extended hands of warmth. We graciously welcomed their presence. The detectives had already spoken with the attending physician earlier, obtaining permission to speak with his patient, but given instructions not to overwhelm him. Agreeing to respect the doctor's orders, the officers got a green light to proceed.

Settling down for a round of questions, but before starting, Jemison gave extended sympathy to my father for the horrific pain he had endured: going a step further, he promised they would not give up until the culprit had been prosecuted. Holmes concurred.

A short while later after the interview began, the detectives realized my father did not remember much about the events on the day of his injury. Although disappointed, the two detectives were happy to know he would have a strong recovery, and live a full, productive life, all because the bullet trajectory went through the right frontal lobe tip, above the skull base, leaving behind only mild damage.

When the meeting was coming to a close, the door open, alerting all to extend their undivided attention toward the large slab of wood.

Suddenly appearing in the doorway was a group of familiar faces known to me, and my father. Immediately I got up from my seat to greet the unexpected visitors who were members of a church where my father was once the pastor and allow the lady to sit down. Tagging along behind them was my sister Trinity who had become a regular visitor, along with Taylor, and Chandler.

Soon the detectives got up from their seats; preparing to leave they extended their goodbyes, reassuring us the investigation will be top priority. Shaking my hand as they departed, Detective Holmes stated, "since we didn't get a chance, please tell your father thanks, we appreciate his cooperation, and hopefully the next time we see him it's on the other side of these hospital walls." Promising I would relay these sentiments to him, they turned, left the room, and closed the door behind them.

Time marched on without concerns of our family's problems, but meanwhile my mother continued to reek havoc on all who were not siding with her, causing troubles to brew inside hers and Trinity's, estranged relationship.

Preparing for another visit to the hospital, Trinity had become upset; calling me on the telephone screaming in high vocals, declaring war on Kandi, she demanded my full, undivided attention. With all greeting being a complete oversight, she plunged into her points of disapproval, speaking absolute disdain for our mother's way of thinking. "She has lost her mind, and so have I for listening to her rhetoric all these years; years I can't retrieve! I've wasted my life on nothing, trying to help in what I thought was something. Your mother had the audacity to come to my apartment today pretending to mend fences of lost time, and hosting thoughts of including daddy. You know what Junior...I believed her! I didn't think she could let me down any further than the day she stood on the side of Thomas after I told her he raped me: twice, but today she proved me wrong. Anyway she doesn't matter, because through God's loving stabilization and the greatest man He could have created to live on this earth, has helped me find peace. If it had not been for God and our dad, I would have lost my mind, or no longer living to talk with you today. Because of them, today is not about destroying my life, but living it. On the other hand, I've had thought about being found guilty and spending some time in prison for the murder of Kandi Douglas Mallory, our family, Judas Iscariot! But knowing God has gifted my life back to me and this will not please Him, or daddy, she'll live!"

I desired to give an ovation behind her statements, shouting from the amen corner, but Trinity left no room for audience appreciation, during her hostile, solo performance about our mother.

"I had no thoughts of her being able to reach any lower in her protective measures for that disgusting animal, disguised as a man. When I opened the door, the smell of trouble should have been overwhelming, but being induced by mixed feeling, I swung open the door so wide, it hit the back wall. In many ways I was glad to see her, mainly hoping she had come to apologize for not standing beside me, as well as a possible reunion. Instead, after the novelty of brief happiness had worn off, I crashed, falling down to reality when she announced her true reason for being there. After releasing our embrace, we went inside to sit; have some fresh, homemade lemonade, but lacking the ability to keep up pretense for very long, soon presenting her other side, breaking the enchanting spell. While holding my hand her face lost its smile, when suddenly her tone became cold, causing my heart to race with fear as she firmly stated, "Trinity, I needed to talk with you about something that's been bothering me." Pausing for a few seconds, she continued, "please tell me....why did you kill Thomas? Trust me, I won't be mad." removing my hand from inside hers, unable to see anything but red after hearing the word trust, it made me more furious than being accused of murder. Seething inside, but with the great desire to be Christ like, I carried the cross of patience, and tolerance.

Staying calm, I stood up, walked toward the same door she enter, and said, "I won't lower my standards as a Christian to even think about transferring filth onto my hands from a dirty, low life snake like Thomas Laskey, not even to kill him. Now if you don't mind, I have to prepare myself to go to the hospital to be with people who love me, people who won't falsely accuse me of a heinous, vicious crime."

"I knew the truth would hurt, put you on defense. A guiltless person would not react the way you are reacting."

"Just how am I reacting?"

"Guilty! If you weren't, you wouldn't be in such a hurry to get rid of me. I must have struck a nerve. And since you know what I'm saying is true, all you have to do is go to the police and confess. Don't hide behind denial, it will eventually destroy you. If you like, I will be more than glad to help you get through this. It will make it easier if someone is in your corner." Standing in the doorway beside me, looking into my eyes with a serious glare of emptiness, she proceeded to tell me while holding my shoulders in her hands, "the reason I ask you about the murder, someone from Thomas neighborhood has brought it to my attention that they saw you leaving his home that's conducive to the timeline of his death. Please, if you turn yourself in, the system will have mercy on you, and so will God."

"How would you know what God would do? When was the last time you even spoke with Him? As far as being in my corner, I'd rather you be in the corner you stood in after learning that lunatic raped me!"

"Being ugly won't help you. If you won't accept my help, which is totally up to you, just do what's right. By the way, I've spoken with God more than you'll ever know, or believe, especially since you're breaking the fifth, sixth and seventh commandments."

"How would you know what I've broken, did someone tell you? Lady.....never forget to always remember, you shouldn't sit in judgment of anyone when you have broken all of the commandments, especially the first."

"Trinity, you are so disrespectful! Well, I guess you have decided to be on your own when the police knock on your door, but know this, once you open the door, the law will handcuff and lead you away for life. It's best to make the move first, before they can make theirs."

"Know this, if that times does come, I will never walk the journey alone, because I have a God who loves and knows me. I also have His people who will walk with me through whatever may come."

"Suit yourself, but a brother, and father is nothing like having a mother at your side. Something the average young lady would desire most of all, in all situation."

"Well, I'm no different than the average young lady, so when you see my mother tell her to give me a call, or better yet, give her my address. Again, if you don't mind, I need to get dressed so I can leave for the hospital."

Disgusted with me, because I did not fall for her entrapping confessional, I patiently waited for her to finish slow walking across the door's threshold to make her final, welcomed exit. Eventually standing outside of my home, I slammed shut the wooden divider standing between us.

Immediately, I thanked God for revealing to me the ways of the wicked that came to steal, kill and destroy. Shortly thereafter while getting dressed, I began feeling

Brenda M. Files

sorry for the lost, lonely lady, but soon laughed out loud for concerning myself with someone who was no longer human, even if she is my mother. Right now, I'm thankful to God the drama is over, so sorry for my delay to get to the hospital, but I'm on my way! Hey...I also want to visit Terrance, okay!"

"Okay! And sorry you had such a dramatic morning; I'll see you soon."

Only a few seconds had passed when the telephone rang again: however, this time it was Taylor. Before I could say a word, she pounced with a voice of excitement, a sound I had not heard from her in a very long time. "Hello, one of my favorite people in the whole world, after God, Terrence, and your dad! How's everything going?"

"Hello, one of my favorite people in the whole world! Everything is good, particularly when you sound so great."

"I sound great for some unknown, strange reason, but it feels good! Well, I was just calling to let you know I will be there soon to visit, afterwards we will go together to see your brother, okay."

"Okay! By the way, before I forget, Trinity will not only be at the hospital to visit our father, but she has also decided tag along to visit Terrence. This morning she became highly motivated through encouragement of unforeseen circumstances, causing her to release all inhibitions of seeing her brother behind bars!"

"Awww heck, there goes my perfect high of great feelings! What happened?

"I tell you what.....wait until Trinity is here so she can tell you, because I couldn't do it justice. I'm sure she'll be glad to repeat it. Besides, there's someone else here that needs to hear it as well."

"Well, one thing is for sure, I am on my way; just don't start the party without me."

"There is no way we can do that; everyone knows, no party would be complete without you!"

We chuckled, then hung up the telephone.

About a half hour later, Trinity arrived. Opening the door, she peeped inside to reveal only a glimpse of her eye; reminding me of her antic when we were children. Surprising both of us; in a thunderous, deep voice, my father cried out a demand, "get your silly self in here!" Without hesitation she complied, rushing swiftly over to the chair where the hospital staff had assisted him to sit, (now a daily part of his physical therapy). After giving him a loving kiss, Trinity threw her arms around his neck, weeping; gently holding onto their embrace, because this was the first time she had seen him sitting in a chair.

Still holding her position, Taylor entered the room and immediately became overwhelmed by the sight of pure love displayed between father, and daughter.

"What's going on in here?! I thought the party wouldn't start without me!" she said with enthusiasm."

Releasing our father, Trinity took her forearm to dry all evidence of water from her face and finally found the ability to greet Taylor. "Hello there Miss lady!" sniffling, she continued verbalizing her feeling. "You caught us at a vulnerable moment. I was just so shocked to see my father sitting up like the champion he is; instantly I became filled with joyful emotions!"

"I understand, because your brother, and I had the same reaction to this beautiful sight last night," Taylor stated, with tears caressing her long lashes.

The room became filled with infectious love, but once all was calm again, Trinity shared in explosive animation,

Brenda M. Files

the entire, ugly morning she spent with her mother; demonstrating with facial disfigurement, the re-enactment of Kandi's pathetic performance. Filled with uncontrollable laughter, everyone pleaded for her to stop. Later, in serious conversation, my sister, and dad gave their undivided attention to everything Taylor, and I had to share with them: the information, Sam shared with us about the supposed death of Peggy, and attempted suicide of our father.

When all the details had been laid out on the table, Trinity became totally speechless; something she had never been in her life, except during her recovery from the horrific experience Thomas forced upon her. Taylor suggested we discuss this situation with Terrance, and Diamond as soon as possible, to hear their opinion about turning evidence over to the detectives. Casting our votes, everyone agreed, including our father, to wait on our siblings opinions.

Now, we were all guilty of committing crimes; obstruction of justice and withholding evidence, both punishable by law. Regardless, we bombarded Diamond's answering machine with urgent messages: believing she would not be in agreement, but compelled to stick with our mother....right, or wrong.

Early the next morning; no longer having a strong relationship with our mother as agreed with Terrance, Trinity, Taylor, and my father, I gave Kandi a phone call to give her the opportunity of knowing the entire story of what was going on with the new evidence police had uncovered. We were giving her the same courtesy she had given her children; turn herself in to the police, pray for leniency, and reminding her.....they will be coming with handcuff soon. Surprised at her next move, I became motionless. Kandi began begging for a few days extension, to get her business in order before involving the police. Purposely I didn't answer, or tell her we were waiting to hear from Diamond, not for her sake, but for my sister's opinion. I wanted Kandi to squirm, even if I couldn't see her reaction.

I found myself gloating over her frighten vocal expression concerning her inevitable fate, and for the first time in a long time, Kandi would finally feel the pain of separation, and loneliness, once justice start breathing down her neck. She'll also find no one standing by her side.

Meanwhile, Taylor, more boisterous than everyone else, introduced to us a very understandable reaction. "I'm starting not to like this! What if she tries to run, escape from the law, what happens then?"

"I pray she wouldn't do that, she has already brought enough harm to her life," my father said. Hearing his sympathetic tone, I knew he wanted nothing but the best for her; still having love for the past life they once shared as he sat in his recliner with sadness drawn on his face.

"Well, one thing for sure, I want someone to pay for the murder of my mother, and since my rapist is no longer available, the one who really should be punished, I'll settle for you guys mother. I want that low down cow to be brought to justice, future escapee, or not. And no matter how long it take, her legs can't out run the law forever. Please know this, I will not apologize to anyone for what I called her, I'm just expressing the way I truly feel. To tell the truth, it's not the name I really had in mind for Kandi," Taylor scoffed.

Trinity in protest, began spilling the unsaid words of others. "Well, unlike all of you, unequivocally I'm a firm believer, you should call a spade a spade! Taylor, I believe the name you are searching for is heifer! There are no apologies deemed necessary for her heiferish, if this is a

Brenda M. Files

word, witchy behavior. The lady is a heifer, not a mother. If you want to hear the truth, I don't give a good flying flip if anyone becomes angry with me for anything I have to say about, or against her. When she stopped caring, so did I! Please people, don't tell me I shouldn't feel this way, because she is still my mother. Hear me family and hear me well, I will not defend myself against statements I make against her, including when I say, she is a real mother for ya! Now don't get it twisted, I love her, because God loves me; however, I'm afraid if I am up close, and personal with Kandi it would put my heavenly chances at risk. I'll never grant room enough, or give her the chance of that being taken from me!

After only a moment of silence in the room, Taylor declared loudly, "y'all better continue your prays for me, because I'm not close to heaven yet! Truth is, I want to kick her behind, hang her by the toes, stick a pole with large splinters down her throat, pull it through the stomach, break it off in her butt, and watch death take over slowly, then gladly take my allotted position in hell!" causing everyone to burst out in laughter. A second later, my father said, "Amen!" Inducing even more laughter.

CHAPTER SEVENTEEN

A s hours evaporated from the clock, Diamond arrived at our mother's home for a short visit. No longer living with her; now sharing an apartment with Chandler, she entered into the home, to find a distraught person reeling in despair from devastating news about her upcoming future. Immediately Diamond ran over, sat next to her on the sofa to extend loving comfort and a needed shoulder to cry on.

"What's wrong mother? What happened to make you so upset?"

Shattered, the valves on her water flow opened to full blast, releasing the growing, uncomfortable pressure lodged deep within. Allowing Kandi a few moment to gather her emotions, Diamond remained motionless, saying nothing.

Silence filled the room, other than the sound of sniffles, and the clearing of nostrils, minutes passed away before Kandi had the ability to speak. Taking her time between the annoying interruptions of quick breaths from constant whimpers, and hic-cup laced words, she reached over, grab her daughter's hand, placed it inside of her, looked into her eyes and spoke in a low tone.

"There are some things you need to know that's been kept secret, and you need to hear it from me. Before you were born your father, and I had marital problems: problems I always blamed him for, but the truth is, I am the one to blame for everything, including the collapse of our marriage. For years, after becoming a successful officer in the military, I was resentful, ashamed of being married to a non-commissioned soldier, often calling him, less than. I knew he loved me with all of his heart, and soul, but somewhere down the line, I had fallen out of love with him. Cringing at the thought of his touch, I wanted him out of

Brenda M. Files

my life! I wanted him out of the state! I wanted him out of the military! I wanted him dead! But we had committed treason against the Army throughout our military careers, therefore, in the end I knew his secrets were my secrets; his stay in the military was my stay, no matter the title we held."

Releasing her daughter's hand, Kandi got up, walked across the room, stood in front of the fireplace with her back turned, listening to the crackling of the fire and watching its flickering flames dance in the dimly lit room; unable to look at Diamond, she continued sharing the gory detail of what had been hidden for so many years.

"When I had my children, they became the joy of my life, but it was not until I truly fell in love, had my lovers children did I really find real joy and love. The man I fell in love with was, Thomas Laskey and the children he gave me, are you, and Terrance." Terror filled Kandi's entire body. "I couldn't tell you, or anyone else, because he had a family, and we had so much to lose. No one, including your father knew the two of you weren't his biological children; just like our marriage, I carried secrets vaulted from many including, Charles. We agreed to separate in order to save our careers, to protect our family from rumors, and gossip. However, I didn't want to just remain separated, I wanted a divorce; I wanted official documents. Although Charles disagreed, eventually he relented; giving any needed papers for me to have my freedom. On the other hand, Peggy refused to sign, or give thought to the idea of divorcing Thomas, binding him to a loveless marriage forever. But needless to say, we never stopped loving, or seeing one another. There was nothing, or anyone who had the ability to stop what was meant be."

Finally dismissing the fireplace from her view, Kandi turned around to look into her daughter's face,

"You see Diamond, Thomas, and I were soul mates, we were finally at the point where we would be together without hiding our love, we were finally going to be married. I was going to be Mrs. Thomas Laskey, but this happiness was taken away from me when Thomas rejected Terrance as his biological son; killing him in heated anger."

Walking across the room once again, she sat down on the sofa, placed her hand on top of Diamond's, stating, "I hope you understand, I love Thomas, and the gifts he gave me. Don't get me wrong, I love Trinity and Junior, but to have true love blended into one to create living beings, elevated everything onto a higher level. Sometimes, the extra attention I would give to you and Terrance was due to the fact; you two were not able to be with your real father. I felt a great need to compensate for his absence, substituting the imbalance in your lives with extra love. Trinity would sometimes become combative against my extra closeness to you; leaving me with no words to explain the complicated situation, because she wouldn't understand. Junior, didn't seem to care either way; he was always being a big brother, or somewhere trying to emulate, or please Charles. I'm not sorry I was more drawn to the two of you, but as far as I'm concerned, I wasn't as physically, or mentally dedicated to the man I created Trinity, and Junior with. Trinity felt inferior to you, due to your features, hair texture......"

Interrupting the ammunition of insults ready to be fired toward her sister, Diamond decided she had heard enough, and needed to take a stance. Removing Kandi's hand from hers, this time she stood up, walked a few step across the floor, then turned to look into her mother's face, ready to wage war in a tongue battle. "I've heard enough of your rhetoric, I can't take anymore. Now, it's my turn to speak, and you just listen." Startled by the declaration, Kandi did as she was told, permitting Diamond to sound off in anger.

"Having to sit here listening to you say things that should have been said over twenty years ago has come far too late. Maybe, if you had said something yesterday it would be different, but it's only when you're facing possible prison time you've decide to be transparent."

Looking bewildered, Kandi wondered what Diamond had been told. Extremely frighten by the unknown, she said nothing, while the canals of her eyes allowed water to flow down her face. "I know more than you think. If it had not been for my real mother keeping me posted I would still be in the dark, ignorant just like you wanted; possibly a target for Thomas. You see my real mother, but at all times I call her Trinity, has kept me abreast of everything happening in this family."

"Trinity is a liar, you can't believe anything she says."

"Please be quiet, and don't make me ask you again; if you do, I'll just leave. You don't get to say negatives about Trinity, and think I'll remain in your presence. If it had not been for her and my real dad, I wouldn't really know, or remember how true love should make me feel. So, contrary to popular belief, Charles Mallory is my father: he has always made me feel loved. Until one day, after you fell into a hot, lusty bed of heated adultery, to quench your needs, you decided to send him away behind lies. Then you come home, brainwashed us, particularly me, to help you treat him as the enemy. You deliberately armed us with disrespect, and anger, creating thick malice in my heart. You made it difficult, if not impossible for him to show me love, and I helped. But now you don't have the right to disfigure either one of them in front of me ever again."

Unable to refrain any longer, Kandi stated, "Diamond you don't understand the power of love, or understand, I didn't try to hurt anyone. I just wanted my peace of heaven down here on earth; peace Thomas gave to me. He gave me treasures, he gave me you, he gave me Terrence."

Getting up from the sofa to walk over to her daughter to extend an embrace, immediately she was rejected, when Diamond walked away, moving further across the floor, almost reaching the entrance of another room, folding her arms in front of her body, signaling separation, making a stance of not wanting any physical connections with the woman perpetrating as a mother. Having disapproval as her only power and friend, Kandi began filling in any gray areas with vivid colors of known reality, while fighting the tears continuing to steadily flow, without permission.

Diamond stood there for a several minutes looking with disdain, before saying a word. "What Thomas has given you is a lifetime of imprisonment, filled with pain, and loneliness. He has enlisted you to live in Satan's hell, after giving you what you thought was heaven on earth. Believe me when I tell you.....there is nothing you can say, or do that will ever make me understand the road you took, to destroy our family, or separate me from the love I knew. Now, allow me to tell you about the trail of horror you left behind for your family to clean up."

Sitting down in the chair nearest to where she stood, Diamond started to peel open the insanity of her past life; living in the home with her mother.

"Unfortunately for me, the place you left for me, and Terrence is a place called, 'lost'. Yes, I noticed there was a vast difference between mine and Terrence skin, hair and eye color, compared to our sister and brother. As a matter of fact, after meeting Taylor, and Chandler in school, most students commenting on how much we looked liked sisters; two plus two actually added up to four. This addition summed up the confusion; answering lingering questions you, and Thomas created for me. I can't speak for Terrance; we rarely discussed personal thoughts about our family's dirty little secrets. Instead, we allowed ourselves to be smothered with happiness; receiving love from our daddy, Charles Mallory. A man I want to....if he will, be my father again, a man I want to smothered me in his love, a man I hope one day will forgive me for my stupidity, and accept me back into the fold as his daughter, even though I don't deserve it. Again, that's why you can't degrade his character, or speak negative about him in front of me. For a few moments, in the beginning of telling your truth, you started out being honest about yours, and Thomas behavior against our family, making me respect you as a person, and mother, suddenly you turned the table, placing blame on others; enveloping Trinity also into your failure of being honest, or a mother. The saddest part of it all, I allowed it! Well, no more."

Before making her way over to the sofa to have a seat, Kandi opened her mouth to defend her honor, but when Diamond saw this action, she immediately stopped the utterance of any words.

"Are you deliberately being obtuse? Like I respectfully ask before, please don't interrupt me; I have the floor. It's my turn now, so hush, or I will walk out!"

Closing her opened mouth, she took heed to the strong demand delivered by her daughter.

"The only things these two people ever did in my life is protect me, something you failed to do. I'll bet you didn't know that Mrs. Peggy, after learning of mine, and Terrance existence, found a way through her children to become close, treating us as if we were from her own blood. During this course of understanding she never gave a hint, or clue about the continued maleficent between you, and Thomas. She was a class act, a wonderful person. Once I learned the two of you had taken her away from me, destroyed the innocence of my sisters Taylor, and Trinity, I wanted vindication for them, even if they didn't seek it for themselves. The feeling of dislike you planted inside of me against my real father, has now transferred on to you lady."

Suddenly, Kandi resembled a deer in the middle of the road caught in headlights, but remembered to remain quiet.

"Being disappointed in most of my misguided ways, I am truly grateful when it comes to my real, and extended family, Taylor and Chandler, especially since I am about to tell you something that you will not like, but you will have heard it from the horse's mouth. As I became closer to Taylor, and Chandler something happened that we are not ashamed of....I fell in love with Candler and she's in love with me. We have been in love for a very long time! Twisted isn't it. This is the outcome of what secrets will do. I'm sure it's hard to hear that your daughter is gay. The same way it was for the infamous Thomas when he heard the news. It was impossible for him to handle the thought of two gay daughter's, who happens to be in love with each other: a very bitter pill for him to swallow without water. However, when we told Mrs. Peggy, she accepted the relationship; helping us to close out the sound of any negative vocals. She knew we had been through enough in our lives, and decided to help us live positive for the rest of it, in whatever manner she could."

Pausing for a few moments, Diamond looked down at her hands and the floor, giving Kandi time to wonder how she knew so many details about all the terrible things she and Thomas had done. Trapped in agony, she remained silent. Finding the strength through all of the negative feeling for her mother, she finished laying out the real truth as she knew it.

"When I learned what Thomas had done to Trinity, was the tipping point, but to find out Thomas was the cause of my father being in a coma, sent me over the edge. That's why I went to his home to let him know how much I hated the two of you for creating me. When I arrived, he was walking you to your car, displaying inappropriate behavior, through passionate kissing in public. Instantly, I lost my mind. A few seconds later, he waved goodbye cheerfully as you drove down the street into the darkness; I watched your taillights travel down the road, waiting for you to turn the corner, vanishing from sight. Once you disappeared, my attention was drawn back to Thomas. Hurriedly I crossed the street, stood on his front porch, rang the doorbell, and waited on him to answer. Giving no thought, he swung open the door jovially expecting you to be standing on the other side, returning for one more kiss. Suddenly his face became filled with disappointment when he saw me standing on his doormat; immediately he began questioning my reason for being there."

"Where in the hell did you come from? Where did you find the guts to come to my home? What do you want?"

"From your hellish seed! To see if I'm your daughter!"

"You mean, my son!"

Turning to go back inside, he purposely left the door open for me to follow, I voluntarily accepted.

"Thank you for answering me about being the man who impregnated my mother with a seed to create me."

"Whatever makes you happy. Now what else do you want to know?"

"Are you Terrance father also?"

"Yes I am Terrance, Taylor's, and Chandler's father, and a few other bratty bastard's running around the grounds of cities, and Army bases,!

Anything else?"

"Yes! Why did you chose to backstab your assistant, your friend, my real father? He trusted you with everything, including his wife, and both of you betrayed him."

"I don't have to answer anything about Charles, or anyone else you ask me about, including the question about yourself. Although, I will say this about your dad as you call him, he is no man at all if he can't handle his family's business. He's even less than a man to have a confused boy, girl come here to stand in the gap for him."

"My dad is more man than you can ever think to be, even more of a man than you could ever try to become. He is a man that took your bullet to the head, but still lives. He is a man who raised your children, he knew were not his. He stands tall as a manly father. He is a man who lost his wife, and family to lies, but still forgives. He is a man that knows you are a rapist, and a murderer, but still held your secret. Now tell me, what's your description of a man? Is it you? an adulterous, raping, murdering coward!

Permitting a few moments to pass Thomas started to slowly walk across the large room toward me with a look of evil drawn all over his face; instead of waiting to see if he was coming over to give me a hug, or a fatherly kiss on the cheek, without giving a second thought, I pulled from my pocket the gun I brought with me for safe protection. Unfazed by the weapon of defense aimed at him, Thomas began walking faster. With his arms stretched forward, his finger curled, resembling Herman monster, I became fearful of his unpredictability, and took a few steps backwards. In an effort to deescalate the situation, speaking in a peaceful tone, I told him to please calm down, before something is done we may regret.

After this efforts didn't work, I tried calling his name, hoping to break his trance, but to no avail. Becoming overwhelmingly nervous by the impossible situation, I pulled the trigger of the gun without awareness of how many times the weapon had fired during the gripping action of my finger on the trigger. It wasn't until the whole ordeal was over, I finally heard the repeated clicking sound of the empty gun's hammer snapping against its frame.

Now totally aware after waking from my trance, I saw my world of reality, Thomas lying on the floor, bloody, and his body riddled with bullets holes. I knew without question, I was the cause of this horrific scene, but at that point, I didn't know what I felt about him possibly being dead. In the meantime, I celebrated for a host of people who was wondering if justice would ever come for him.

I became startled when the dogs started barking in the background, causing me to hastily move my feet in rapid pace toward the closest exit. Once outside, fear over powered all of my thoughts, bringing on memory loss, even the walk back to my car was not remembered, recalling only the moments I drove down highway one-ten, headed home.

The next day, surprise engulfed my every thought, when I learned Terrance had also gone to Thomas' home on the same day. After seeing Thomas on the floor bleeding, he ran, but unfortunately for my brother there were eye witnesses identifying him as the person fleeing the scene. Later the detectives came and arrested him for the murder of Thomas; I was devastated. I rushed to visit him in jail without anyone else being aware; I wanted him and him alone to know what happened the night Thomas Laskey was killed. After hearing me say, "I have a confession to make," and a sorrowful look in my eyes, he quickly told me to go home, talk to no one, especially him while he was in jail. Reminding me before I left, "jails, and prisons hold no secret, so be careful of all actions, and things spoken when visiting." I took heed.

However, the night before seeing him, I had already decided to carry out my exit plan for Thomas, leaving you mother as his murderer and the attempted murderer of my dad. You see, the gun belonging to you is the same gun Thomas stole, and tried to kill my father with, now it has killed him. After arriving at your home, where I was still living at the time, I saw him wiping the weapon clean when he came back from visiting my father: however, he had no idea I was watching every move he made. Underhandedly, he went into your bedroom, taped the gun on the back of your nightstand while you were in the kitchen preparing him dinner. When he left the room, I retrieved the weapon for later use, and since we both knew you never carried the gun, believing you wouldn't realize it was missing; his escape plan from you was set in motion; also my plan for him. He used your gun in case the two of you were pitted against each other; automatically he would declare his innocence, pointing all fingers in your direction. The love of your life was prepared not only to blame you for the attempted murder on my father, but also Peggy's. I know this, because he wrote it down.

Ballistic will prove the fatal bullet that killed Thomas, and hurt my father, came from the same gun the police will find in your home. They will learn the gun found next to my dad's injured body, after reexamination of the bullet, didn't come from his weapon, but a perfect match to yours.

Brenda M. Files

They will also find the bloody jacket, and shoes worn on the night of Thomas death, both belonging to you. These item will unfortunately for you, have Thomas blood splatters on them, not to mention, the gunshot residue; gifts from me. In the end, my brother Terrance will have his freedom again, since he didn't do anything but find a low life, dead man's body. Happily, we will watch you finally get what you deserve. I just hate Thomas isn't here to share a life in prison with you, or be escorted down the corridor to the death chamber, next to the love of his life."

Shocked by the things her daughter was saying, the length she had gone to carry out this plan, Kandi asked, "Tell me why would you do this to me, your own mother?"

"I will tell you, if you tell me where my mother is located? I need to ask her why were all of these horrible things done to so many people? I will tell you, when you tell me why she tried to destroy my father, and why she took away a lady that was a real mother to me? If you tell me why, I'll tell you why. In the meantime, please don't waste your time looking for your gun, jacket or shoes, you'll never find them, but I can guarantee, the police detectives will. Stricken with grief, the only thing Kandi could find to say was, "Diamond, I don't deserve this!"

You're right, you don't! You deserve only death, where there will never be the possibility of parole." A few minutes later Diamond turned, and walked out of Kandi's home, leaving her behind without a thought, or guilt.

A day later, our father was finally home from the hospital. The same day he came home, Diamond, Taylor, Trinity, as well as myself, decided to follow through with our plans. We called Detectives Holmes and Jemison, asking them to meet us at my father's home as soon as possible...they agreed. Immediately after hanging up the phone, I picked it up again, calling Chandler, asking her to come over, and bring Amy with her. Excited, she accepted, for both of them. About an hour later everyone had arrived, the house had become filled with many conversations flowing at one time, every light in the house glowing brightly and laughter dominating the atmosphere, because the time had come for everyone to file into the dining room to share a happy family reunion, and a long awaited, delicious meal together. Shortly thereafter the detective was prepared to indict my mother on multiple crimes, including murder after picking up and reviewing all evidence we gave to them. Armed with an arrest, and search warrant, they set out to pick her up. In the meantime, me and my family gathered around the man we all loved, celebrating his homecoming. However, the most important thing was seeing Diamond sitting next to him holding his hands, not wanting to let go, because she was finally home.

Unfortunately, about three hours later the telephone rang, it was Detective Jemison on the other end of the line, informing me that our mother was missing, believed to have fled the country. Quickly placing the officer on the speaker phone so all could hear, he reassured us an all points bulletin had been put in place for her apprehension; she is now declared a fugitive on the run, promising us "she would be caught." Before hanging up the telephone, she calmly stated some good news, "we're on the way to drop Terrance off at your father's home to complete your celebration."

Shortly thereafter I found sitting alone, Taylor looking unhappy, had become sadden about the news of Kandi's escape, because she had been reluctant for extended time before turning her over to the police. But soon thereafter, she relinquished the thoughts of Kandi when she saw all of

Brenda M. Files

the joyous smiles around the room, celebrating a good man. This brought me pleasure. Later I saw Trinity looking at Diamond smiling as if they had a family secret of their own; when suddenly for some strange reason, I began wondering if Kandi was missing on her own accord to be found later by police, or missing never to be heard from again. In the end, I never questioned my sister's to learn if they knew of her whereabouts, because at that time it really didn't matter, the only thing that mattered, was today and our innocent brother would be coming home, a place where he too belong. Hours later, Trinity found her way over to Diamond, grabbed her hand, leading her out to the outdoors and soon the two were traveling down the steps, for a brisk walk to a secluded escape for a sisterly chat. In the meantime the rest of the family continued the celebration without wonder of their disappearance. It was a day that had been filled with beautiful sunshine, but now as the dusk of evening prepared for the darkness of night, they continued walking arm in arm while taking the narrow path to the park. Listening and enjoying the sounds in the background of nature's rustling leaves, whistling winds and birds chirping high pitched, soprano notes, harmonizing together song of happiness, the two sister's continued moving forward with no real destination in mind when Diamond caused both of them to stop in their tracks to asked her sister a question, "now that Thomas is dead, no longer around to bother you, what are we going to do about his and your baby?" Trinity didn't reply, she just fell into her sister's arms, and wept.

MYSTICAL POWER

I am a woman of mystical power,
A magnitude of justification,
I am days of grace.
I am captivating and celebrated,
Tapped into a waterfall of exceptional strength
Strapped to discipline,
Bound by determination.
I am captivating, and celebrated
Giving birth to unlimited growth,
Producing multitudes of wondrous sensations.
How wondrous is my celebration.
Never shaken by waves of turbulence
Standing in devastation, and afflictions
Enduring shattered hopes, and dreams
While continuing my golden stairs journey,
Never ceasing my climb, because
I am a captivating, and celebrated woman.
I am a woman of mystical power
I am days of amazing grace
I am God's wonderful creation!

Brenda M. Files

SECRET GARDEN

You picked me up, placed me on your trusted knee,
You took away my childhood of being carefree.
You looked inside my private flowered place,
And took away fun games, my hopscotch space.
You are family, my uncle, father, a close friend,
You unlocked my treasure and forcefully entered in.
I close my eyes to wish you, and the pain away,
But now with secrets, other children I won't play.
God where are You? Why am I left alone here?
Have I been such a bad girl to live in this fear?
Lord, You gave me this garden of pure love,
Your gift is tarnished, no flight of my dove.
Please Lord I pray, lock my garden door,
But today, inside my innocence he'll soar.
I wonder if his attention for me will ever cease,
I'll just place my mind in a place to find peace.